THE ASIAN POWER LEAGUE

力

THE
ASIAN
POWER
LEAGUE

力

DR. GLENN TOBY

Indigo River Publishing

Indigo River Publishing
3 West Garden Street, Ste. 718
Pensacola, FL 32502
www.indigoriverpublishing.com

Asian Power League | Glenn Toby, author
ISBN: 978-1-950906-61-1 | LCCN: 2020943758
Edited by Joshua Owens
Cover and design by Robin Vuchnich

Special discounts are available on quantity purchases by corporations, associations, and others. For details, contact the publisher at the address above.

Orders by US trade bookstores and wholesalers: Please contact the publisher at the address above.

With Indigo River Publishing, you can always expect great books, strong voices, and meaningful messages. Most importantly, you'll always find . . . words worth reading.

Dedicated to my loving mother, Winifred A. Weems,
who drafted the blueprint of my lifework with the gift of education,
and in honor of my brother Randall E. Toby and Judith J. Weems.

Special thanks to my spiritual brother Dan Vega
and the Indigo River Publishing family,
as well as David Matthew Branch and Jevonte McCall,
for adding power to my dream factory!

CHAPTER ONE

The Blueprint

THE SUN WAS SETTING OVER MANHATTAN during rush hour. In a state-of-the-art luxury office building, the staff of Hy-Yung & Associates were busy at work. David Hy-Yung, the middle-aged man who built this billion-dollar empire in the import-export business, was going through another fast-paced day in the life of a business mogul, struggling to remain a fixture in his young son Michael's life, a very bright and hyperactive three-year-old. David was sitting on the floor playing a word game on his computer with Michael and the daughter of his best friend, who was a diplomat, a little girl named Kimjianta, whom he was babysitting this week. The telephones were ringing off the hook when three executives entered the room and tried to talk with him, but he refused to stop playing with his son.

"Sir, I need you to sign these papers. It's urgent. The deal is nearly closed," said the female executive.

"Look, the deal will have to wait. My son is three years old, and I am not about to miss some of the most precious years of his life," replied David.

"Sir, believe me, I can appreciate what you're saying, but we have a deadline. Please just sign here and I'll be out of your way," replied the woman, pointing to the documents on her clipboard.

"OK, OK"—he stood and signed the presented document—"but everything else will have to wait until tomorrow. Do me a favor: have Peter bring the car around. It's getting late."

One of the executives mumbled under his breath with impatience and aggravation, realizing this delay would not just cause great disappointment to his team but could potentially prevent them from closing the deal they were working on.

As the three executives left the room along with Michael's father, who had to return little Kimjianta to her nanny, David stopped and turned around to say, "Michael, say goodbye to your friend Kimjianta. She has to go back home now."

Michael stared at her with a sad face and refused to return her wave and smile with anything but disappointment, and then looked down at his feet. Kimjianta again said goodbye while she walked away, and Michael was taken to the car by their chauffeur, Peter. After Peter had put on his seatbelt and returned to the driver's seat, he glanced in the rearview mirror at Michael sitting in the darkened backseat of the SUV.

The boy heard Peter as he thought aloud: "Shit, you're gonna have the world in the palm of your hands by the time you're eighteen years old, kid."

"Shit! You shit!" Michael said, letting out a little boy's roar of laughter.

"Hey, little Mike, don't say that. Those are bad words."

"Shit you!" Michael cackled with laughter. "Shit! Shit!"

"Don't say bad words, OK?" repeated the chauffeur. "If you don't say bad words, I'll let you drive."

"OK, OK, Peter."

Peter got out of the car and opened Michael's door. He pulled him out of the car and placed him in the front seat, where Michael began to play with the steering wheel. "Mike, you sit next to me and let me drive," Peter said, then picked him up and placed him in the passenger's seat. They drove around the block a few times, and as they returned to the front of the building, the boy's father was waiting. Peter stopped the car and let him in.

"Son, come sit in the back with Daddy," said David.

"Mr. Hy-Yung, he wanted to drive. This boy is so ambitious," said Peter.

"Trust me, I know. Now come here, son. Leave Peter alone so he can drive."

Michael crawled over the seat into the back and said, "Daddy, Pete is gonna drive for me. I want him to drive for me."

"You got it, big guy. I'll drive for you, but you got to be drinking age or I'm gonna stick with your dad," Peter said, as both men chuckled.

CHAPTER TWO

The Foundation

Michael Hy-Yung—now twenty years old—was standing in front of the library of the college he attended, speaking to his friend John McNamara.

"Michael, are you familiar with an organization called the Young Pioneers of America?" John asked.

"I've heard about them. They're like the Freemasons or Skull and Bones, right?"

"Not quite, Mike. Let me explain."

"OK, tell me more about them."

"I wouldn't call it a secret organization, but I can't go too deep into specifics. Let's just say it's a group of unique men that is committed to building and sharing the American dream," John said. "Mike, I wanted to talk to you about joining. We need someone like you to help us change the Pioneers' image and give it more of a modern platform. I mean, we're in the digital age."

"What is the mission of this organization?" Michael asked.

"It's a fraternal order for us, the youth of today," John replied. "We believe that, in order to rule the world tomorrow, we must start today. We have supporters and sponsors all around the world."

"Are you guys very well financed or deeply connected? How did you go about it?" asked Michael.

"Mike, you have to understand that people see the Young Pioneers of America as an insurance policy for a free world. It's a secret organization that has been around for decades. The FBI viewed us as subversive and counterproductive and thought we were Communist in the past."

"Well, how did you survive?" asked Michael. "How did you guys get support and turn everything around?"

"The president of the United States pulled a few strings. Once he got into office, he used his influence to help us reinvent the organization."

"I must admit that you guys sound very powerful."

"Yeah, Mike, our alumni includes ten former United States presidents, hundreds of Fortune 500 CEOs, and countless heads of state. This would really be good for you."

"Well, I would need to learn more about the organization before I would consider becoming a member."

"I understand, Mike. We would love to have you as a member. There's a meeting this afternoon. You should come by and learn more about it. Give it a chance, and if it's for you, I would be more than happy to nominate you to pledge for membership. Our group believes that you can be a critical part of us rebuilding this local chapter of the organization."

"Where is the meeting place? Do I need a password or something?"

"No, of course not, but it's by invite only. We have reserved the student activities lounge conference room. It isn't a big secret. Only the alumni meetings are top secret. So be there at two p.m."

"I have an economics class at twelve forty-five. I won't get out until two o'clock."

"Don't worry. Just get there as soon as you can."

"Cool, I'll see you then," said Michael.

***

Later that afternoon, John spoke passionately to the members of the organization.

"Good afternoon, Young Pioneers. I would like to introduce you to a true pioneer and an excellent example of a good American citizen, and a model student. Michael, would you be kind enough to come here and allow me to introduce you, please?"

Michael rushed over to stand with John as he spoke.

"This is Michael Hy-Yung. You have seen him on television, magazines, talk shows—everywhere. He has expressed a sincere interest in our organization, and I believe, with all my heart, he would be a great candidate for membership and should join our organization immediately. He has the pedigree and character to be nominated for the office of the chapter president."

The crowd mumbled in shock.

"Wait, wait—quiet down now. Next semester, I graduate, and due to the limited time that I have left, I can no longer serve this office. I would like Michael Hy-Yung to be accepted into the Young Pioneers of America and one day assume the office of president," said John.

It was no surprise that Michael was being nominated quickly to take over as president. He spent most of his time on campus either in his dorm or in the student union attending hackathons and guest speaker events. In all things Michael spoke on, he showed how voracious a reader and extensive a researcher he was. His passion and commitment to his studies, club activities, and the overall college lifestyle allowed him to create his own world on campus, which had drawn the attention of many powerful figures on campus.

"Speech, speech, speech," chanted the audience as they applauded Michael.

Michael cleared his throat and spoke from his heart: "I am honored to be nominated, and I am hopeful that my member-ship will be approved by you all. However, if I am to accept this membership and the possible appointment of president one day, I will only do so under one condition"—he paused—"and that is we start holding elections and end the process of appointment, as you are considering with me. Let's have a Young Pioneers of America election in the next thirty days and start the beginning of a new era." Michael walked into the crowd to greet the stu-dents and shake hands.

***

Thirty days later, Michael was at the Pioneers meeting in the student lounge once again, after being elected president of the elite club and changing many of the organization's rules and regulations. Standing in front of the audience, he was prepared to make his announcement accepting the office of president.

"I am proud to be the president and leader of this chapter of the Young Pioneers of America. Our organization will represent the ideals and dreams of the pioneers and great contributors of the past. I'm talking about the greatest minds that have ever lived. It is our responsibility to renew faith and instill the fire and compassion that we once had in this country for peace, love, strength, morality, and the great things this country has to offer to all Americans. But this time we must work to make sure that no one is excluded from the promise or the process."

The crowd applauded as Michael stepped down and walked away with John.

"Mike, there is one thing you must remember. You have access to anything and everything you need. Just make sure you deliver when the Pioneers call on you."

"Sounds fair to me. I know I have what it takes."

"Very well. I am certain that this is going to work, for all of us."

Michael divided his time between college life and activities and building a research-based quantum-stock-trading platform. He had developed unique software that enabled him to generate data that gave him an edge in evaluating equities, bonds, and debt instruments—a system that quickly allowed him to create massive profits, which made his name one in the ears of many executives around the country even though he was still in college.

CHAPTER THREE

The Team

THE ORGANIZATION WAS CALLED "THE TEAM," a group of highly accomplished men and women, based all around the world, who were extraordinarily secretive, wealthy, and powerful. They brought value in one or several categories: academics, engineering, technology, mathematics, philosophy, medicine, business, politics, or religion; or they could be thought leaders and trendsetters in the creative world. As a group, they had the power to change popular trends in culture and thought, or the behavior of society as a whole.

Members who did not have wealth, or were not born into influence and power, had created or could invent a product, service, or thought process that brought value or resources to the Team. It was the responsibility of each member to work together regardless of a member's age, race, ethnicity, religion, sexual orientation, or opinion. The goal was to provide an idea, or perform an act, or bring a resource that would give them leverage over the entire world. This required that every member remain loyal and proactive. The Team had created a system that gave them great advantages over the average global citizen, one which allowed each and every Team member to benefit collectively.

Government investigators discussing the Team often used the analogy of each member being like an athlete in a major sports league, such as the New York Yankees or the Dallas Cowboys. Law enforcement agencies and government administrations around the world considered this dangerous group of men and women a team of players in a league named the Asian Power League.

The Asian Power League was just that, a best-in-class group that was committed to changing the planet at any cost. They were playing and building a new world for and by themselves. What made the league so unique was that no one could find documentation of its true origin. Some scholars said it was started in China at the beginning of civilization and had evolved to become a more sophisticated and structured organization over the centuries to match modern society.

Law enforcement around the world consistently reported that the Asian Power League was a more recent organization started by the Japanese to overpower the United States and gain control over American citizens. Supposedly, their actions were in response to the horrors that many Asian Americans had suffered by being placed in internment camps during World War II, and the period of rampant racism against the

Japanese, and the Asian community at large, as a result of the bombings that occurred at Pearl Harbor.

Of course, there was speculation it was headquartered in a different country in Asia in order to provide the group—and its original founders and creators of this doctrine—anonymity as they operated and built the membership base from within the United States and other countries all over the world. It was clear to all investigators that no one outside the organization truly knew where the Asian Power League started, but many were praying for its end.

CHAPTER FOUR

Access Granted

GRADUATION DAY HAD ARRIVED. Michael Hy-Yung had just finished talking with job recruiters. Letters and printed emails were scattered amid unopened computer boxes, brief-cases, and other perks around his room. He showered, got dressed, and rushed to the campus bookstore to meet Mark Chatham, a recruiting agent that Michael's parents hired to represent him and get him the best employment deal.

Michael's private car was already waiting for them.

Michael had grown cautious and started strategically planning his meetings for his safety. He gave his trusted driver instructions to drive around Georgetown and downtown Washington, D.C., until he said otherwise. He rarely met with anyone outside of his inner circle face-to-face anymore. It was even rarer that he met with someone outside of that circle at all.

Once the custom black Escalade with tinted windows pulled away, the driver rolled up the partition between the seats to provide Michael and Mark privacy.

"Michael, there is a program that has just been launched, and it will require your honesty, commitment, and ultimate secrecy," said Mark.

Mark was a forty-five-year-old athletically built British gentleman. He was class valedictorian many years ago and had been considered a potential candidate for a brilliant career in politics. However, he had no desire for public office. Best of all, he was also Michael's college advisor.

"Mark, I'm your man, but I want full control. And when I produce results there should be no questions asked."

"Michael, if you can bring your theories and concepts to life, you will rule with autonomy."

"What's the catch? What do I have to do? I mean, who gets all this shit without something fishy being involved?" Michael asked.

"There are no strings attached. If you turn profits, you rule with absolute power. No questions asked. The more you achieve, the more you receive. You will only answer to God himself," Mark said. "You will be in utopia—a complete vacuum without anyone or anything standing in your way. All of your problems will be taken care of, and anything you ask will be arranged for by the board."

"Come on, strings always tie things together. Who is on the board? Who's funding this program?"

"Michael, stop worrying. Governors, mayors, lawyers, doctors, universities, churches and synagogues, and especially my favorite: the private sector. You never know—it could be the president of the United States."

The car pulled over when Michael rapped on the partition three times, and stopped to let Mark out.

As he exited the vehicle, Mark said, "Now, enough talk. Read the program, give it some serious thought, and call me if you're interested."

Michael took the briefcase with the documents in it and returned to his dorm. He studied every page over and over, using his iPad to do independent research online. He made phone calls and sent emails to friends and associates to gain a better understanding of the nature of the deal. Michael finally read all the documents before falling into a deep and well-warranted sleep.

***

On graduation day, the president of the United States of America was the guest speaker for the commencement ceremony.

After the president's address, Michael joined him on stage. The president shook his hand and introduced him to the crowd as the class valedictorian and an example of a model citizen of the United States of America. Michael took the scroll from the president and approached the podium to deliver his speech.

"Today, I would like to thank you all for your trust and your commitment to the world leadership education program here at our university. This great program has given me the opportunity to attend the finest scholarship program ever created. Our university studies have given us all the chance to compete with the greatest minds in the world. Today, there are no losers, just winners. But still, I will not be victorious until my mission is complete. That mission is to contribute and continue to build until we have all the members of the human race sharing the gifts and rewards that life has to offer us in every facet of life. I have not won. I have been chosen by you to lead and represent the collective efforts of bringing mankind together. So, I say to the doctors, lawyers, political leaders, and my fellow students: let us begin today to win the ultimate challenge of defeating evil, suffering, and pain by using our minds and hearts to start a new world."

The audience went into a mad frenzy as Michael walked off the stage. They rose from their seats in a standing ovation, and many members of the audience, including a few senators and congressmen, walked over and surrounded him. The president of the United States gave Michael a thumbs-up and a wink as he was ushered into the presidential limousine.

As the motorcade pulled off, Michael and his roommate, John, talked on the side of the crowded stage.

John turned to Michael and said, "Come on, Mike, let's get away from this crowd quick, man. We need to talk."

Michael was slightly nervous and had a look of great concern on his face. He was always supportive of his roommate and had been a generally easygoing team player and friend. "OK, let's go to the monuments," he said.

The two walked away from the excitement to the other side of campus and sat down in front of the statues of Presidents Lincoln, Washington, Kennedy, Roosevelt, and FDR. Both young men were still wearing their caps and gowns and were in a pensive mood.

"John, you know, sometimes I think it's really gonna happen."

"You think what's really gonna happen?" John replied.

"You know—me . . . becoming the president of the United States."

"I mean, everything is there for you, Mike. You've got senators, governors, judges, and the richest people in the world backing you, along with the YPA. It's gonna be like money in the bank for you later in life. Just concentrate on business. Politics is just a tool."

Michael had gained tremendous popularity and access to clubs, events, and activities that introduced him to prominent alumni and ambitious students who had engaged with him and invited him into their circles.

"Yeah, but tools fix things that are broken."

"Then don't fix things that aren't broken. Stick to business."

"John, everything is so perfect. What's missing?"

"Things are perfect now, but anything can change in twenty years. Besides, one thing that will never change—"

"Yeah, yeah, yeah," interrupted Michael. "I'm Asian, right? But you said it, John: political platforms are only tools to build or destroy broken systems. I'm going to play their game and pimp the system."

"Well, I'm with you, buddy. You haven't failed yet. I have your back until the end. I mean, if a black man can become president, anyone can."

"Thank you, Mr. Vice President, but, damn, that sounds racist. What the hell does that mean?"

"No, just the opposite. It's real life, Mike. It has nothing to do with race, color, or creed. It takes ambition, hard work, and intelligence. Now, cut the bullshit. OK, Mr. Future President, what do you have planned for your next twenty-year campaign?"

"It's a secret. I can't tell you."

"Bullshit! I've got so much dirt on you, I could blackmail you for the rest of your life!"

"True, but don't forget that I was videotaping you the night you pledged for your fraternity," Michael said as they chuckled.

"Mike, you've got everything going for you, and you should be very careful of any offers that sound too good."

"Don't worry. Everything has been taken care of."

"Good. I'm sure you made the right decision. I'm just concerned, Mike."

"I am in a selective program. The senators I worked with talked to some people for me, and they created this new program."

"What program are you talking about?" asked John.

"I'm in the Capital Evaluation Program. It's the dream of a lifetime. I can't believe it!"

"Wow! I heard about that. How does it work?"

"I work at a different corporation in a different industry each year for five years, and I have to reach certain goals."

"That means your earnings potential is limited, you're tied down," said John.

"No, my attorneys put in a stipulation that I get a percentage of all the profits and financial gains the companies receive from my programs and projects."

"What happens after the five-year period? Are you free to try the open market?"

"I'm going to retire and start my own company. I even have a name and concept for the company. Listen to this—"

"Hold it! That's private. I don't even want to hear about it," John said.

"Slow down, man. It's just an idea! Everything is trade-marked and set up. This is fact, not theory, and my advisors are just waiting for my command."

John and Michael broke out laughing like two schoolboys.

"Alright, alright, let's hear your idea," said John.

"I'm going to name the company the International Financial Development Corporation. I'll be a hired gun for any company that is failing or going bankrupt. I will turn them around to a profit position," replied Michael.

"And what are you gonna get?"

"I'll receive a percentage of profits and equity in the companies' ownership."

"That's asking a lot, isn't it?"

"That's a bargain. It's me or bankruptcy, dude. I'm their only chance. I'm going to change the world when all my theories are put into practice."

"Well, Mike, I'm headed to London. I'll be with Heather and Plaxthorn, Limited, of England. They offered me the position of vice president of business development."

"Great! I'm gonna need you, so stay in touch."

"Here come your folks, Mike. I'm going to give you guys some privacy."

John hugged Michael's parents as he was leaving. When they walked over to Michael, they had tears in their eyes. He greeted his parents as they all embraced.

"Son, I am so proud of you. What did I do to deserve becoming so fortunate? You are a miracle."

"Oh, Dad, thank you. I am the one who has the greatest blessing in the world. You and Mom have given me so much."

"Darling, thank you for giving us so much in return," replied Michael's mother.

"Mother, you and Dad poured your entire lives into me. I just can't believe my whole life. You mapped my every move up until this moment. You opened the doors. I just had to follow the road you paved for me."

Michael walked with his parents back to their car and kissed his mother goodbye.

His father said, "You have done everything we asked of you, and we are pleased."

David Hy-Yung was a very healthy man for most of his life. Michael remembered his dad as a man who had worked tirelessly without drinking or ever catching a cold, so his suffering with a major illness was beyond belief. Over the past few years his dad had been struggling with a rare health disorder. During that time, Michael had assembled a dream team of the best doctors, researchers, and health-care facilities around the world to create a protocol that would cure him. This personalized medical plan included a baseline blood test and was supported with herbs and ancient Asian medical modalities. This protocol had brought his father great relief and delayed the progression of this serious disease, but of course it could not prevent the inevitable.

"Dad, is there anything else I can do for you? Dad, I know—"

"Know what?"

"I know about your recent prognosis. I spoke with Doctor Calaberi. He told me everything."

"Son, it's OK. I may live longer than anyone knows."

"Well, Dad, my friends are part of a group of scientists that is developing a treatment protocol that may cure your disease.

They're in the final stages of clinical trials, and a great deal of the research has been very successful. They're reporting that it has a ninety percent efficacy. Let me send you to the clinic again for treatment. The director has approved you and guaranteed me that he will care for you directly."

"No, son, please respect my wishes."

"OK, Dad. I just want to know, if there was one thing I could do to please you, what would it be?"

"You've done everything a father could ever ask and pray for. You must follow your true destiny and what's right, Michael. Join the Asian Power League. There are great treasures for you there. Our family heritage shaped the organization. They have great power. It is time you let them know who you are."

Michael's dad had told him stories of the Asian Power League when he was growing up. The APL had seemed like an elite social club of old men back then. Years later, Michael realized it was a powerful corporate machine run by a group of wealthy men and women who were some of the most ruthless and brilliant minds in Asia. They operated in secrecy and silence.

David Hy-Yung got in the car after he hugged his son. Michael smiled and waved as his parents drove away.

Later Michael was in his dormitory room packing the last of his belongings in preparation to leave. He reached for his phone to make a call.

"Give me Mark Chatham, please. It's Michael Hy-Yung from American University."

There was a brief silence before Mark picked up the call. "OK, Michael. You have to run a profit at each company you serve each year," Mark said.

"Mark, where's the challenge? That's my game, profit, baby."

"You see, Michael, our key people will be trusting you with their lives. If you are a winner, you will have the world in your hands, no holds barred and no restrictions. Michael, let's talk in the morning."

"Sure thing, Mark. I'll see you tomorrow."

CHAPTER FIVE

The Assignment

FOUR YEARS HAD PASSED, and Michael Hy-Yung began his fifth and final year of the internship program at Clark Industries. He had developed a great reputation as a solutions-based team member who brought resolve and innovation to every challenge presented to him, earning the respect of everyone from his colleagues to the CEOs of the companies he had previously worked with. His track record put him in a position of strength that often led to bidding wars for his services.

A couple of executives were standing near one of their computers trying to solve a major problem with a portfolio of companies that were on the brink of bankruptcy. If these companies failed the valuation, the entire enterprise would be compromised. That the chairman of the company had assigned

Michael to this particular project spoke volumes about his talent and maturity. In the event Michael turned it around, he would not only be über-wealthy, but he would become a mythical character credited with one of the greatest corporate turnarounds in American business history. One of the executives suggested they ask Michael to assist them in solving their problem.

"Hey, Dale, let's assign Hy-Yung to the debt restructuring project. Let him do all the work. We'll tell him it's for research. Then we take all the credit for ourselves. It's the American way. This report could take years," he said.

"Adam, these are complicated equations. We will have serious problems, and if Hy-Yung screws it up, they will not only get rid of him but us as well!"

"Dale, let's just call the chairman and tell him that Hy-Yung asked to be involved in the project and that he demanded we give him an equal chance to resolve the issues."

Dale quietly mulled the idea over in his mind before saying, "Then we will have to get him interested in it and set him up after he accepts the assignment."

"After we give him the project, we'll tell him that it's not that important, it's just something we were all curious about, like a mock training assignment or an experiment," said Adam.

"After he reviews it, he will see how difficult the situation is. He will know that this is real," Dale said. "The guy is brilliant, and besides, he may find out that the chairman is stealing from the company."

"It won't matter if he does. When he returns the assignment to us, we'll change everything around and turn it in as our work and take the credit," said Adam.

The next morning at the office, Adam and Dale took their opportunity to introduce themselves to Michael.

"Hi, I'm Adam Bright."

"And I'm Dale Stevens."

"Pleased to meet you. I'm Michael Hy-Yung."

"Dale and I are the coordinators for the project that you're assigned to. We have heard great things about you, and we've watched you build your career. We wish you the best. You have our full support."

"Thank you very much. I'm fully prepared to start. Is there anything in particular you request of me during my term with you?" Michael asked.

"No, nothing at all. You will be working on an assignment-by-assignment basis. The workload varies, but the choice of selection doesn't. You must accept and fully complete any and every assignment we give you. Upon the completion of all the projects, you will be granted your certificate of completion in the program," said Adam.

"And one other thing: this is all top secret information, and we would appreciate it if you kept everything confidential," Dale explained.

"Very well, I'll get started now," replied Michael. With a shake of his head, he took the flash drive that Adam extended to him and walked briskly back to his office to begin work on the first project.

CHAPTER SIX

Karma Calls

MICHAEL HY-YUNG HAD OFTEN STRUGGLED with the ethics and principles of traditional corporate practices and standards. He had told his parents as a youth that he wanted to be an honest man who made billions of dollars and still kept his soul.

The chairman of Clark Industries was deeply involved in several corporate acquisitions, mergers, and block trades that were improper at best. Michael was well aware of the improper transactions, as well as the possible breach of fiduciary responsibility that was built into the business systems; they had brought him many sleepless nights. Michael also knew the Securities and Exchange Commission was doing an informal inquiry into many of the CEO's past dealings, but no previous deals or questionable transactions could be used against him—the statute of limitations had expired. It was Michael's duty to navigate the CEO around any litigation or criminal prosecution. If he could protect the chief executive officer and transition the company into the future, it would make him the man with the Midas touch. With a careful and well-executed plan, he would eventually become the heir to the throne of a new and long-lasting dynasty.

Six months had passed since Adam and Dale's initial exchange with Michael. Adam and Dale, still slightly overweight and just as deceitful, called Michael in to meet with them.

As Michael stood inside this ultramodern office, he tried to concentrate on keeping his mind in the moment. The room was the most modern, tech-styled office he had ever seen. There were computers everywhere, blended with precious artwork and collectibles. As one of the executives began to speak, Michael struggled to focus on what he was saying.

"Hy-Yung, I am sure that you are aware the project you are involved in is just a mock and that none of this is real. It's just a hypothetical exercise to keep our minds sharp," said Dale. "I mean, we are the most successful company in our industry.

"And though the report was not due for another four months, you have finished it in just six," he continued. "I will personally see to it that you are offered a job or given a letter of recommendation, because our staff relies on our young interns like you to stay ahead of the competition. Without people like you, we wouldn't be able to succeed."

"You mean fuck people over and hold them down? Come on! Did you really think I was that stupid? I know that report is real!" said Michael.

"What are you talking about? This was just a training exercise to expose you to corporate fraud and show you how things can go wrong," Adam tried to say convincingly.

"Hy-Yung, you keep running your mouth and you'll be suspended from the program and I'll make sure you're blacklisted," Dale threatened.

At that moment, Chairman Langston Clark's voice boomed through the intercom: "Gentlemen, can I see you in my office, please?" The question was more like an order. The men walked to the chairman's office, quickly and silently.

As Michael, Dale, and Adam walked into the room, they could feel the power and sincerity of the men present. Each of them had a mysterious, yet familiar, vibe about him. They had obviously been discussing something urgent.

Michael was suddenly overcome with a rush of euphoria that almost knocked him to the floor. He saw his life flash by him as he imagined himself surrounded by attorneys, bodyguards, and a room full of reporters and photographers. He envisioned himself as the president of the United States of America in that moment. It seemed real. The moment of déjà vu seemed to last a lifetime.

"Mr. Clark, we got your message, sir," Michael said.

"Senior Vice President Adam Bright and Executive Vice President Dale Stevens, I would like to inform you of your termination from Clark Industries without pay and without pension! I would like you both to leave this industry for five years, and if you do not leave the state of New York, I will be forced to take further action," said Mr. Clark.

"I don't understand, sir. This is quite a hardline approach!" exclaimed Adam.

"Sir, we knew there was a chance you would find out what we did to Hy-Yung, but that was only to protect you, sir, from any implications and to ensure that no one could trace the embezzlement," Dale added.

"If you had any concern for me, you would never have given sensitive information like that to anyone. You're risking our entire operation. Not to mention bringing the kid into this shit. You set him up. This would have destroyed his entire career. He was considered a national hero for turning these companies around and preventing them from going into bankruptcy. If those companies had failed, it would have been a disaster to the world economy and left a mark on some of the most successful businessmen of the last four decades."

"You're right, sir. We're very sorry to have jeopardized everyone. Hy-Yung, I hope you accept my apology. I meant no harm," said Adam.

"You're kidding. The both of you aren't smart enough to frame me," replied Michael.

"Is there anything we can do now to make this right?"

"No, Dale, there isn't! You should pack your things and get out of town. It seems like someone did some research, and the private investigator we hired as a result told us you guys are the embezzlers. If you stay quiet for seven years, you're free to go your own way," snapped Mr. Clark.

"You can't do that. It's not fair," said Dale.

"Shut up! Are you crazy, Dale? Mr. Clark, I think you are being more than fair," said Adam.

"Just sign these documents and follow the directions of my attorneys and you will have no problems."

Adam and Dale sat down to sign the documents and endured the lecture given by the lawyers, who advised them on how to stay out of trouble.

Dale tried to appeal to Mr. Clark one last time: "Could you please give us our last paycheck now that you're going to take our pensions and company benefits? We won't have enough to support our families. Can you let us have something?"

"Yes—you're leaving with your life. Now get out of my damn sight!"

Michael headed back to his office as Dale and Adam were escorted out of the building.

***

It was sunny and warm the next day when Michael returned to the office. He stepped onto the elevator but wasn't paying attention and got off on the wrong floor. As he turned to get back on the elevator, he heard a familiar voice. It was Mr. Clark, who was surprised to see him. He invited Michael into his office to chat.

"Have a seat, Hy-Yung. I just want you to know that we are very pleased to have you here with us. How have things been going for you?"

"I really enjoy it here, sir. I have learned a great deal, and it's wonderful being an important member on such a successful team."

Mr. Clark reached into the bottom right drawer of his desk for Michael's file and set it on his desk. Reading through it carefully, he grinned. His freshly cut white hair glistened under the fluorescent lights of his office.

"Hy-Yung, you are truly a remarkable and gifted individual. You could not have performed any better under these circumstances. You have gone above and beyond the requirements of everything you've been involved in. What has been your most rewarding accomplishment since interning with us?"

Michael cleared his throat before responding. "Well, sir, handling the restructuring project and working with the private clients in the company have been a thrill and an honor. I'm honored to have created the formula that saved the company, sir."

As he glanced once more through the files, it became apparent that Mr. Clark was taken aback. He dropped the file on his desk and stood up from his chair. He was a tall, wide man and seemed to loom over Michael once he made his way around the desk to face him. He grabbed Michael by the shoulders and said, "Hy-Yung, I know you are well aware of what's going on, and not only have you brought the company back to a solid position, but you have not reported what I was doing and your system covered all of my transactions. Thank you for your loyalty. I will remain in debt to you for as long as I live. Remember, the key to the game is loyalty, kid."

CHAPTER SEVEN

The Launch

MARK CHATHAM AND MICHAEL were having a conversation in the backstage area of the university auditorium. Michael had returned to campus to visit faculty members and enjoy a few group organizations and events.

"It's bonus time today, Mark," said Michael assuredly. "I completed my term. My five years are up, and if you don't have any other great deals for me, then I have one for you, buddy."

"Well, Mike, I would like to make you an offer to join my new corporation. You will be my key advisor and second-in-command. Here's my proposal," Mark said, handing Michael a manila envelope. "Read it while I get ready for the ceremony."

Michael accepted the folder and reached into his backpack for a brochure on his own company, which he handed to Mark. As he buttoned his shirt, Mark read through the brochure and smiled and nodded approvingly.

"Well, Mark, are you thinking about joining me today or tomorrow?"

"Yesterday, Mike."

"Great! I'll inform the staff tonight that you're my COO and you will be second-in-command," Michael said while tying his tie.

"Very well, Mike. Let's go. The press is waiting on you. I'll still make the opening speech."

The Young Pioneers of America had rebranded and created an aggressive recruiting campaign targeting young, brilliant students. The leadership had decided they would be open and inviting to the public at large. From what Michael could see of the crowd, the Pioneers had succeeded in their mission.

"OK, come on, everybody! The world awaits us," Michael said over his shoulder to his entourage of twenty. The group then made its way to the auditorium stage.

"Ladies and gentlemen, we are here to celebrate a great moment in education and business. A very special program has come to an end, and a great business era has begun. It is the start of Michael Hy-Yung's career. After successfully completing the Capital Evaluation Program, he is about to embark on a major project of his own. And now, on behalf of the Young Pioneers of America and American University, we present the one and only Mr. Michael Hy-Yung!"

As Michael approached the stage, cameras could be heard snapping and several members of the media emerged from the crowd to get clear shots. Michael approached the podium with confidence and power, surrounded by an army of his supporters and dedicated associates.

"I would like to announce the start of a new company: the International Financial Development Corporation. Our company is made up of the greatest minds on earth, and we propose to turn any bankrupt company or failing company into a flourishing gem. We have a strict and demanding list of requirements. For any corporation to become our client, it must meet certain financial requirements and pass our stringent interview process."

A reporter in the crowd spoke out: "Mr. Hy-Yung, what are you expecting in return for your services?"

"We request a percentage of equity and equal participation in the profits of the company."

"What is the profile of your average client?"

"These are companies with billions of dollars in assets and brilliant employees, and we are focusing on companies that are in dire straits."

"Mr. Hy-Yung, I take it you will be the messiah of the corporate world, or the savior of the economy," a TV reporter called out.

"No titles, sir, just results. We want the big companies that the free world depends on to flourish and keep the world economy strong. We are hired mercenaries fighting for the economic freedom of all and helping to prevent the collapse of our global economic system. Thank you for your time, ladies and gentlemen. Have a great day."

Michael and his entourage took their exit and headed back to their Wall Street offices.

CHAPTER EIGHT

Bulletproof Business

FOR THE LAST YEAR AND A HALF, Michael had been on fire. He had gained international notoriety and was constantly pursued for employment opportunities, joint venture deals, and partnerships.

"Mr. Tenner, I would love to be more involved in this deal, but I can't. There is no way I could be more objective on the matter. Besides, there's a conflict of interest and it's against the law," Michael said.

"Against the law? Against the law my ass!" Mr. Tenner replied. "Your whole empire was built on payoffs and underhanded deals."

"Those are some strong accusations you are making. I am never directly involved in any deals made by the company. If you believe something was done improperly or the law was broken, tell me and I will order a full investigation."

"Mr. Hy-Yung, help us out and we will make arrangements to give you an even greater deal than you wanted," Mr. Tenner said. He put a proposal on Michael's desk.

"Mr. Tenner, why should I get involved? I get a million deals across my desk every day."

"We gave you your first major financing on the Dunbar Holdings merger deal. We gave you an unlimited credit line and transferred billions into your personal accounts. We were your personal piggy bank."

"Very true, Mr. Tenner."

"We gave you your start. We financed your dreams, and you bought our bank and squeezed it for every fucking dime and left us broke and busted."

"Mr. Tenner, your approach to this is emotional and biased. This is a business, not a fucking marriage. I value all of you and I am well aware of the doors you have opened for me. But I still had to walk through them, so get up off your fucking knees and be a man. What can I do for you?"

"I read the memo you wrote for the employees, and I know that you are going to fire the entire staff and use your bank to run ours," Mr. Tenner said. "Well, sir, if it's not too much to ask, could you loan each employee a year's salary for severance pay and another year's salary as a loan to be paid over five years? Now, bear in mind, some employees have been at the bank for over twenty-five years."

"Twenty-five years or twenty-five minutes," Hy-Yung responded. "It doesn't make a difference. I just took over yesterday afternoon, and I'm not going to inherit your burdens. Here's the way it is: six months' pay to each employee at their current earnings rate as of today, and all loans must be filed the same way our customers apply—of course, with our same rate and high standards. But to be honest, Mr. Tenner, I don't think they will be approved."

"Why not, Mr. Hy-Yung?"

"Because they're unemployed."

"You son of a—"

"Mr. Tenner, I am very sensitive. Don't upset me, or I'll be forced to change my mind, or worse—kick your little ass."

Mr. Tenner became enraged and headed for the office door, shouting over his shoulder, "You have obviously forgotten everything!"

Michael got up and threw the proposal at Mr. Tenner as he walked out, shouting, "No, you forgot something!"

Michael then called his receptionist on the intercom. "Jenny, send in the next appointment."

CHAPTER NINE

Order and Oath

LATER THAT DAY, RICHARD GOLDMAN, Michael's executive assistant, abruptly rushed through the door of Michael's office. It was filled with unpacked boxes, mail, and FedEx and UPS packages. Documents cluttered the space; awards and framed photos lined the walls. Luggage, shopping bags from luxury-brand boutiques, and wrapped gifts were piled in the corner near the window.

Michael believed that corporate and municipal funding should be used with modesty and spent with common sense.

Richard Goldman was frantically yelling as he approached Hy-Yung: "We can't get through to Yodhkhan, and the company will not acknowledge our offer. Who is this fucking guy? We offered him ten times what he's asking for!"

"He is the leader of an organization called the Asian Power League. If I can become an honorary member, Richard, maybe I can make him an offer," Michael replied.

"How do you know they will accept your offer?"

"Trust me, Richard. It's the only way."

"How can you be sure of that?"

"My friends and family have done business with the Asian Power League for years, and they have members in every facet of business and government over there. I mean real power."

"Well, maybe we can find another way to approach him," Richard said. Richard was a long-trusted confidant and a childhood friend. The Goldman family and the Hy-Yung family had done major deals over the years. Richard and Michael grew up together and considered each other brothers.

"You don't understand. This is a secret order that started ages ago, during the time of the great emperors. There are heads of state involved. The whole damn system operates by their rules and methods. The Asian Power League controls all major government contracts, stock trades, and real estate deals. They control half of the entire Asian economy. They have judges, ambassadors, doctors, lawyers, and a who's who list of billionaires."

Though they had been considered a social group with world leaders that had no impact on anything more that social and cultural issues, many people now believed the Asian Power League was the next secret organization to rule the Asian world.

"You mean a syndicate?" Richard asked.

"Man, I mean a government that is run like a syndicate, only bigger and faster than the fucking mafia, the triads, or the yakuza. It's a system—a way of life."

"Michael, if you pull this off, you will become the greatest business mind of all time. Make a contact, give them what they want."

"I have a contact already. I'll take care of it."

As Richard left, Michael picked up the phone and called his cousin Misu Mori. He told Misu that he was coming to Japan to accept the Emperor's Grace Award and wanted to meet with him.

***

After Michael was escorted from his business-class seat to the VIP lounge in the airport, he found Misu greeting him with a bow and saying, "Ah, my favorite famous cousin. Welcome home, Hy-Yung. It's so good to see you. Now tell me, what really brings you here?"

"Hello, Misu!" Michael exclaimed. "I need your help. I want to officially join the Asian Power League. I have the biggest deal of my life depending on it."

"What does a deal have to do with the Asian Power League?" Miso asked.

"The Asian Power League—you know—Yodhkhan. You can't do a deal without him. I need to join."

"Hy-Yung, this is a very serious thing, you know. I mean, it's not a one-time deal."

"Look at my background. Look at my abilities. Look at what I have to offer."

"It is not a question of ability. It is your honor you must prove."

"Look, Misu, just do this one thing for me. I can't go any further without it. I need to meet with Yodhkhan. He won't even talk to me unless I am a member of the Asian Power League."

"That's true. But this is an Asian tradition."

"I am Asian. And our family has had a great impact on Asian culture even before the start of its great rise," pleaded Michael.

"OK, Hy-Yung, I'll introduce you. But there's no guarantee you will get in. We will go to the headquarters after the awards. Then I will go to them and ask to initiate you."

***

At the award ceremony, dramatically and sincerely, Hy-Yung commenced his acceptance speech to a packed audience of several hundred.

"I am honored to receive this award tonight. I would like to accept it in honor of my parents. Our rich Asian heritage has instilled in me the ethics and principles of the Asian people. I have pure Asian blood running through my veins, and I am committed to this great nation. As my mother carried me to America with the spirit of our motherland, I will carry you people and the legacy of our forefathers with me wherever I go, until I die."

Michael concluded his speech, and the audience gave a round of applause. As he left the stage, a woman put an envelope in his pocket and disappeared into the crowd. But Michael had no time to ponder that. He and his cousin embraced warmly, then walked to a dorm on campus and reminisced about the times when they were younger.

Later, when Michael removed the envelope from his pocket, then opened and read it, he realized this was an invite he should consider.

***

Later in the evening, Misu walked over with Michael to a building in which eight figures sat around a conference table. The fraternity members had just finished eating and were drinking heavily.

As Michael looked around, he took in the modern, tech-oriented aesthetic and vibe of this mysterious group's headquarters, not just in its decor and design but in their gestures and culture.

"I would like to introduce you to my cousin Michael Hy-Yung, a Japanese man of high order and discipline. I humbly request that you, elders of the Asian Power League, consider him as a member of your fraternity," Misu stated.

Yodhkhan spoke: "Hy-Yung, as the chairman of the Asian Power League, I would like to nominate you for membership in our brotherhood. We believe you have shown and expressed your abilities and sincerity in helping to develop a better world to live in and grow to power. Do you accept our hand?"

Michael cleared his throat and said, "I have dreamed of one day joining the order, for I have heard great things from my father and uncle of the good deeds and contributions you have made to the world. I would like to offer all that I am and all that I have to you."

"Your theories and formulas have changed the way the world does business. You are one of the most powerful and influential men in the world," Yodhkhan replied dramatically. "Why is it you have chosen to join us?"

"I have conquered many great things in the eyes of man and the business community. However, I believe this is the final step that I must take in order to inherit the full blessings of my parents."

Yodhkhan nodded approvingly and said, "I see that your successes have not had an effect on your ability to appreciate and value life's true treasures."

"Thank you."

"After reviewing your application and doing research on you, Hy-Yung, I believe it is people of your character and ability who will shape this world for a better tomorrow. All those in favor, raise your hands to initiate Hy-Yung into the brotherhood. And those not in favor, do not raise your hands, and explain your reasons, if any."

Everyone raised their hands except for Nuji Misheato, an anti-American, and the woman who had slipped Michael the invitation.

"I think that Hy-Yung is not committed enough to help us establish our position of world domination," Nuji said.

Michael was confused and began to laugh before replying, "'World domination'? That is a strong choice of words!"

"Not half as strong as your actions," Nuji sternly replied.

"Strength is one of my greatest virtues. It is one of the most important ingredients to my winning plan," Michael said, confidently and calmly.

"What is the key to a winning plan, Hy-Yung?"

"My key ingredient is my ability to observe small details. If you read my books or attend my lectures, I am sure you will agree with my system."

"Mr. Hy-Yung, your system and theories are proven, and your methods are needed here. It's just one small detail that prevents me from giving you my vote."

"What's that?" Michael asked.

Nuji pounded her fists on the desk. "Oh, come on!" she exclaimed.

"No, you come on," Michael angrily responded.

"We have read and listened to a great deal of your interviews. I have followed your every move, and didn't you say you were not Japanese, that you were American?"

"I only meant that I am committed to the American people as a whole and that I am undivided. My loyalty is to all citizens of the world."

Nuji was getting argumentative. "Don't you remember all the hate, prejudice, and destruction that America has caused Asian people all around the world? Our people were almost removed from the face of the earth. Many people have died or lost what they had so that your family would have a fortune. You owe respect and a part of your fortune to our motherland. You are forsaking our ancestors and our legacy!"

Michael started to get embarrassed. "I know my ancestors have had to bear pain and suffering. I will not let their sacrifices be in vain."

"How will you do this?" Nuji asked.

Michael lowered his head and said, "I will never allow myself to lose sight of what those before me have done. I am Asian and I am proud of it."

"I can see. You just have a different way of expressing your pride and loyalty," Nuji said sarcastically.

"No, Nuji. I am committed."

"How committed?"

"I will vow to all of my brothers of the Asian Power League that as long as I am alive, I will serve my country and my brothers of this high order. I will help us rise to be the great civilization we were meant to be."

Nuji grunted. "I almost believe you."

"I can't wait to reeducate the world of our greatness and the contributions that the Asian people have made that affect the world. I'm gonna be our modern-day Moses!" said Michael.

"It is true that we have never seen a more qualified candidate," said Nuji.

Michael, emotional now, asked, "Then what still stands before us?"

"I am afraid of your deep love for Western civilization, and your American ways and worship of their icons and beliefs."

"The world pursues riches and greatness with equal valor and desire. I have respect for the world. I yearn only for this last piece in the puzzle of life." Angrily, Michael continued, "Nothing short of death or the calling of God's voice will stop me from serving my people. I would do anything to—"

"To do what? Rewrite history and save the world?" Nuji said, interrupting him.

"I will be prepared to serve and honor our bond at any cost. Nothing can divide us!"

"And nothing will," Yodhkhan said. "Welcome, you are a member. Let the initiation begin!"

Everyone rejoiced. They drank and partied. They also swore Michael in as an official member. Nuji smiled as she watched him walk away with Misu. She whispered something to one of the men next to her before calling out, "Hey, Hy-Yung, I hope you return the favor. I may need your help one day."

"Yeah, you might," Michael responded.

It became late and a Mercedes waited outside. Once the cousins stepped in, the chauffeur rushed them straight to Michael's hotel.

CHAPTER TEN

The Crush

MICHAEL ENTERED A JAPANESE RESTAURANT so popular it could take six months to get into because of its food and the A-list clientele that dined there so frequently. Most of the customers had memberships to reduce the wait. The host seated Michael right by Kimjianta, his elementary school crush. Every summer, when Michael and Kimjianta had visited their relatives in Japan, they would spend all their time together. They had not seen each other in well over a decade.

As Michael hung up his coat and took his seat, he observed Kimjianta staring at him. He felt a rush come over him; he was clearly overwhelmed with emotion and surprise. After years of focusing on his career and building an empire centered on himself, he thought, *I think this woman could be my wife one day.*

"Oh my God, Kimjianta is that you?"

"Yes."

"Why didn't you say hello?" Michael asked.

"Because I was afraid to. I will come over only if you invite me," Kimjianta said.

"Please, come over and have a seat. Do you always follow men around like this and stare at them?"

"No. I only did it once in my life, for a man I truly loved. I thought he could make my dreams come true."

"Then shouldn't you be with him? He sounds like the perfect man."

Michael was moved like never before, wondering if this intimidating beauty was the missing ingredient in his life, or possibly his future wife. He had grown extremely shy over the years, and realized that his social skills were stellar when it came to business, but his ability to communicate on an intimate level was rapidly diminishing. Michael was so nervous and uncomfortable, he was laughing at himself and wondering how he had lost his edge and when it had happened. As nervous as he was, he welcomed the challenge of overcoming himself.

"He left me with a broken heart," said Kimjianta.

"I never meant to break your heart," said Michael. He paused with regret and great embarrassment as he said the most insensitive—and possibly stupid—thing he could say to the woman he wanted to rekindle a relationship with: "What do you want from me? I'm not a genie. I cannot make dreams come true."

"Well, I thought you might be able to make all my fantasies come true."

"Well, I guess anything's possible. You're welcome to spend some time with me," Michael said.

"Good, because I plan to spend a long time with you."

"Do you know what I consider a long time? You can't imagine what I call a long time."

Kimjianta looked down at Michael's lap and said, "That's what I was wondering from the first moment I saw you."

"Well, how curious are you?"

"I'm willing to take my chances."

"Well, they say curiosity killed the cat."

"Meow," Kimjianta purred.

"I'm warning you, it could cost you all nine."

Then Kimjianta handed him keys and wrote her address on a napkin. As she got up to walk away, she said, "Mike, you said nine, right? Did you mean lives, or . . . ?"

"It's a surprise. You'll find out later."

***

Michael had his driver circle the building twice before he entered because he was awestruck by the incredible design of the building, a high-end residential building with a tenant roster that listed some of the wealthiest people in the world. The building, an architectural gem and one of the most revered buildings on earth, was designed to be as functional as it was beautiful. Called a "living structure," the building merged state-of-the-art AI technology with world-class contemporary design. The metal, glass, and other materials used in its construction were designed to be an ecological miracle that would not strain the environment. The firm that designed it just happened to be owned by a company that Michael Hy-Yung owned.

Michael was in the lobby when he heard Kimjianta's voice over the intercom, giving orders to the doorman: "He's fine, let him in."

Michael got on the elevator and Kimjianta was already there, waiting for him.

"I want to make a stop before we go to my apartment," she said.

"OK, I'm all yours," he said.

They got off on the roof, where a table was set for two, with candles and a waiter who kept the food warm. They took their seats.

"Kimjianta, I must admit I have been watching you for a long time."

"Michael, I used to read about you and watch you on TV. I even have a scrapbook on you. You know, one night I dreamed we were married."

"Is that right? Tell me, how was the honeymoon?"

Kimjianta laughed, and said, "Oh, Michael, stop. I'm serious! I have always wanted you for myself. I used to tell Daddy that I was going to marry you one day. In fact, Yodhkhan used to always say, 'Now, that's the kind of man every woman would want to marry.'"

"Did you bring me here to propose to me or to talk about your dad and Yodhkhan?"

After dinner the waiter cleared the table and poured more wine in their glasses. Then he left the roof, locking the door behind him.

"Michael, I brought you here to tell you I want to get to know you better. Who knows, I may end up becoming that special woman in your life. I mean, behind every man there is a strong woman," she said, walking over to kiss him.

Michael responded in a passionate rage. He picked her up and laid her on the table, where they made love.

Later, Kimjianta produced a key to one of the company penthouses' rooftop access. She put her index finger to her mouth and shushed him as she escorted Michael into the apartment. The two lovers headed straight to the bedroom, where they both collapsed.

"Kim, I want you to visit me in New York. I'll make provisions for you."

"Mike, I'm an independent woman. I want to share responsibilities."

"You got it, partner. Fifty-fifty, right?"

"Like business or a marriage," she said.

"Which one would you like?"

"Both, but I don't need a title, Mike. I'm just asking to do the deal."

"Done deal. Let's shake on it."

Kimjianta rolled on top of Michael and they began to make love a second time.

***

The next day, the lovers were still in the apartment.

"I leave in two hours. I don't want you to come to the airport," Michael said.

"OK, honey, I'll stay home if you insist, but I want to join you in New York soon."

"Look, you can do as you please, as long as we are together."

"Michael, I'm here for you and I always will be."

The doorbell rang, and Kimjianta looked out the window and saw a limousine.

"Michael, your driver is here. Have a safe flight and call me when you get in."

"Sure thing, honey. Love ya."

Kimjianta shed a tear as Michael left.

CHAPTER ELEVEN

The Candidate

MICHAEL WAS GREETED BY GOOD NEWS upon his return to the States. In his office on Monday morning, Jenny informed him that he had received thousands of emails and phone calls from supporters all around the world. She also told him of news and TV shows suggesting he run for president. Michael read several newspaper editorials from around the country that were endorsing him for president.

"Mr. Hy-Yung, I have great news for you," Jenny said. "The president of the United States said in an interview that he would endorse you to become the next president!"

"That's an honor, Jenny, but I would have to consolidate my businesses and then sell them before I could run for public office," said Michael.

"No question. That's required of every presidential candidate who's wealthy. Your business manager and accountants can handle that for you," replied Jenny. "The Republican Party leader recommended that you speak with a gentleman by the name of Carl Banner. He's a specialist on these matters."

"OK, Jenny, let's get this thing going. I've always dreamed of being president. I just need a good group of team players."

***

Meanwhile, seven thousand miles away, in the Asian Power League's headquarters, Nuji and Yodhkhan were talking as Kimjianta sat down nearby.

"I have come to realize how valuable Hy-Yung is to the Asian Power League," Nuji said.

"It took twenty years for you to realize this?" Yodhkhan replied.

"Yes—I mean, no. I always knew he was useful."

"Useful? What do you mean, 'useful'?"

"Don't you see? The Asian Power League has the president of the United States of America in the palm of their hands."

"What the hell are you talking about?"

"We will make donations to his campaign and make anonymous offers and contributions to the right people. Without real estate and stock holdings, we can manipulate the marketplace and use leverage to influence and control the key figures in the election. Use our businesses to get support from the unions, politicians, and media. We will control television, radio, and the papers. We can use the press to create hype and propaganda."

"We must be careful. We don't want to do anything to violate any laws, or we will jeopardize Hy-Yung's chance of being president of the United States of America."

"Yes, but we must also do what is right for our people," Nuji said.

"True, but it is very important that we respect Hy-Yung."

"This plan is good for everyone. It will make Hy-Yung president of the United States and save the economic state of the US at the same time. We can take advantage of inside information from Hy-Yung about the government. Imagine the secret information we can get from him to help us rise to power again," said Nuji.

Yodhkhan interrupted: "Nuji, this is insane! It's wicked. I'll have no part of it!"

"We can hire a US publicity firm and get a special-interest group or a lobbyist to influence the key politicians."

"You mean get an American to be our front."

"Even better! We will hire a lobbyist, a senator, or a lawyer. Maybe set up offices, bank accounts, press agents, and spokesmen and then funnel the money to campaign for Hy-Yung."

"We must be careful. The laws are very tight and must be followed closely, or Hy-Yung's presidential campaign will be at risk."

"You see," Nuji said, "we will make donations to his campaign and make anonymous offers and contributions to the right people. With our business contacts, we can influence unions with incentives and bonus money."

"No, Nuji, no. That is out of the question. This is not our business."

"Look, you old fool, you are living in the past. It is time for a new system and new players in this game!"

"What are you saying?" Yodhkhan asked.

"Hy-Yung is good for everyone. He can save the US economy, and we can take advantage of the business opportunities."

"I do not approve of this. It is evil and dangerous. This is the kind of thinking that started World War II and the Holocaust!"

"Yodhkhan, do not stand in the way of progress!"

"You will have to kill me to keep me out of your way!"

"You said it, not me."

"Do what you have to do!"

"No, Yodhkhan. You're going to do what you have to do!"

"Nuji, until you take over, I run the show! Any change will be over my dead body!"

Kimjianta followed Yodhkhan as he walked to the door and then escorted him downstairs to his awaiting limo, which drove him back to his apartment.

**

The next day, Kimjianta feverishly attempted to call Yodhkhan, over and over, because he had missed several appointments in the office. Kimjianta was concerned, so she called Misu and asked if he would go with her to check on him at his apartment.

Misu and Kimjianta went to Yodhkhan's apartment and knocked on the door. Finally, Misu broke the door down and they went in to find that the room had been ransacked and Yodhkhan lying on the bedroom floor, naked. Kimjianta screamed.

"Yodhkhan! Yodhkhan, speak to me. Oh God, no. It can't be."

Misu tried to give Yodhkhan mouth-to-mouth resuscitation and then started to pound his chest, trying to bring him back to life. He then screamed out and broke down into tears. Neighbors heard the screams and came running over.

They called Nuji and asked her to come immediately. When she arrived, she had no expression on her face.

Misu picked up the phone and called the police. When the police arrived, they interviewed several members of the Asian Power League who had heard of the tragedy and come over, as well as Yodhkhan's relatives and other residents of the building.

Nuji seemed to be nervous, a contrast from her usual nonchalance. She sat in the corner observing the scene.

Detective Hiro announced to the group, "We will be in contact with you in a few days, after the investigation has been reviewed by my superiors."

"Do you think you will find the killer, Detective?" Misu asked.

"One can never say. After all, Mr. Yodhkhan was a man of great mystery and power," said Detective Hiro.

"We would like to ask everyone to leave now. We will contact you as soon as the family gets any information," said Misu.

"You are very cold toward me. Is something wrong?" Nuji asked.

"Yes. And don't doubt for one moment that the truth will be known in due time," Misu responded.

"What is there to know?"

"The truth," said Misu.

Detective Hiro cut in: "Excuse me, did you guys go into the apartment with him, or did you see anything unusual?"

"No, sir," Kimjianta said. "I escorted him to his car yesterday. Today I went to the office. I could not reach Yodhkhan all day, and I felt something was suspicious because he missed several appointments today and never called me. I called Misu for my work assignment because I had not heard from Yodhkhan, and I went home at the end of the day. I thought about going over to check on him, but I didn't do it. In fact, I never even went inside his apartment, and I was with my parents when I called Misu. I never left home."

"Let me call Hy-Yung. I know he will want to attend the funeral."

Misu called Michael to inform him of Yodhkhan's death and gave him the information about the funeral arrangements so that he could prepare for his trip back to Japan.

After Michael settled down, he called Misu back to discuss the situation.

"Who do you think is behind this? Everyone thinks it is Nuji, but that would be too obvious. I'm really confused, Hy-Yung. But we have to find the killer," Misu said.

"Nuji is my prime suspect. I think she was involved in Yodhkhan's death. She was acting very strange when I spoke with her on the phone," Michael said.

You know, now that I think of it, Yodhkhan and Nuji were fighting over the direction of the Asian Power League for the last two months."

"What do you mean by 'the direction of the Asian Power League'?"

"You know Nuji. She had ideas and plans that Yodhkhan would not agree to or accept."

"Damn, Misu. How blind can you be?"

"Look, Hy-Yung, we need more than that to go on. You're talking about murder. I feel the same way, but we have to cover our asses. One screwup and we're finished."

"I will be there tomorrow afternoon. I'm leaving on the first plane out of JFK," Michael said.

"OK, Hy-Yung. In the meantime I'm going to do some private work."

Michael got his personal items and called for his driver to take him to the airport.

***

The moment Michael arrived in Japan, Yodhkhan's murder was the most talked-about story in the news, from television to radio to online.

Several thousand people attended Yodhkhan's funeral, including high-ranking Asian officials, US corporate executives, and dignitaries. The ceremony was traditional and mournful. Michael delivered the eulogy.

"Ladies and gentlemen, the Honorable Yodhkhan was a man of resolve and high spiritual fiber. He will be greatly missed. He believed in the balance of power, and now he has been called to meet with the greatest of powers, our ancestors. Yodhkhan believed that all nations are one, and with every gain, there is a loss. His goal was to share the gains with all mankind and remove the losses that humanity must bear. We must enforce and police his ideas so that one day they will be reality. For no one man can uphold such great ideas. We must all work together to continue the dream."

Michael gave Nuji a cold, piercing look as he walked from the podium. She followed him to his car.

"Hello, Hy-Yung. I hope I will be getting your full support in our quest for victory. I assure you, I will be a great leader."

"You are no leader," Michael said. "I do not acknowledge you."

"You are making a great mistake, Hy-Yung. I advise you to make the transition very smoothly."

Michael pushed Nuji out of his way and got in the car.

"I don't think you're truly committed enough," Nuji said. "I never cast my vote for you; I objected your nomination. I don't give a damn what the bylaws say!"

***

It was business as usual at the fraternity headquarters, though the mood was gloomy. Nuji and Misu argued quietly at the back of the hall, while the other members were assembled around the conference table, eating and drinking.

Misu was about to speak, and Nuji walked over to sit next to him.

"Today," Misu began, "we have been forced to accept a new reality and make a change in the divine order of the Asian Power League. The time has now come to officially ordain our new leader. My brothers, by order of tradition and the bylaws of the Asian Power League, Nuji Misheato is our new president and leader. She inherits the position by default from second-in-command to head speaker and chief in command."

Misu extended his hand to Nuji. They embraced and Nuji took the floor to speak.

"Now that our beloved leader has passed, I have been called upon by you, my brothers and sisters, to lead our fellowship to a victorious new day. This is a day of victory in the name of our organization and all people of Asian descent. Our methods will be of brute strength and absolute power. We will conquer and dominate at any cost. Asian people will rise to power and become leaders of the world once again."

Everyone talked and exchanged their opinions as Misu placed a call to Hy-Yung and whispered a coded message on his answering machine.

CHAPTER TWELVE

The Nominee

"MR. HY-YUNG, this is the proper time for you to make your bid for the presidential race. What's standing in your way?" said top political advisor Carl Banner. His pin-striped black suit stood out against the afternoon-sunlit bay window behind him.

Michael answered resolutely, "Well, nothing really, because I know I have the knowledge and the contacts to make my run now. My only concern is getting around the racist bastards that don't want an Asian running the country."

"Michael, we met with all the power brokers that we have. Everyone in the country is behind you. We have enough endorsements to get a presidential nomination. We can hire public relations firms and key media figureheads to get by all that bullshit."

"Well, Carl, if you guys are ready and can put the team together, I'm ready to go. In fact, I want you to head up my campaign."

"Very well, Mr. Hy-Yung. I am going to put together a full-scale plan to get this into motion by the end of the week."

"And I'll make the necessary transition from my business to a full-time politician."

"I'll schedule a press conference for tomorrow morning."

***

The next morning, Michael looked over a massive crowd from his place at the podium before commencing his speech.

"Ladies and gentlemen, after careful consideration and many weeks of planning, I would like to accept the kind offer you have granted me in choosing me as your presidential candidate."

A reporter called out from the crowd: "Mr. Hy-Yung, what is your reason for wanting to enter the political arena?"

"I have always wanted to be president of the United States of America. Since I was ten years old, I have aspired to become the leader of this country, and now I plan to make the best of it," replied Hy-Yung.

Another reporter called out from across the audience: "How do you think being an Asian American will affect your campaign?"

"I believe that America is a rainbow coalition; we have so many nationalities and people of diverse backgrounds. I believe that I represent everyone, and that proves the American dream can come true."

An uproar of applause swept through the crowd as Hy-Yung stepped off the podium into the crowd and greeted people, shaking their hands.

***

Night fell on the national campaign headquarters. In a conference room in the left wing of the building, Michael and Carl Banner, his new campaign manager, were seated at a table, engaged in an intense conversation about political strategy.

"We only have one month left, Michael, and if we keep up this pace, we will win by a landslide."

"I know we will win easily. It's just important to control the media and avoid all bad press and get around any controversial issues," Michael said pensively.

"You're right and we're doing just fine. We've only had one incident thus far."

"What's that?"

"It's not a problem, but we did find large sums of money in the campaign fund bank account three times. However, we are constantly monitoring our affairs, every hour."

"Any idea where the money came from?"

"Yeah, it was from some private group of investors or maybe just a bank error. Everybody is going to try to take credit for helping, but if this money thing brings any heat, we all burn," said Carl.

"We could sure use the money, but we have to go about it the right way," said Michael.

***

Several days had passed, and Michael made his way from his office to the conference room, where he found his campaign manager hard at work with a calculator in one hand and a pen over his notepad in the other.

"I need an update on the polls and a report on our financials," Michael said.

"You're ahead in the polls, but if we can take out more social media ads, we can win by an even larger margin next month."

"You're right, Carl. I think we can blow them off the map if we bury them with an advertising strategy."

"You're doing just fine now. We have to use the issues and your strong background. We are all tapped out and have less than a million bucks left."

"Think of something. We need to raise some cash, fast."

"Well, I'll tell our advisors and the lobbyists who are supporting us."

"Be careful when it comes to money. It could come back to haunt us later."

"Don't worry. I'll do everything I can to stay within the guidelines. I've contacted a guy named Alan Tolsky. He has some big money backers, and he specializes in political and social fundraisers," Carl assured him.

"Go get him. I know you can do it."

CHAPTER THIRTEEN

Gas in the Tank

As CARL BANNER SAT DOWN in the reception area of the office, he could hear the faint sound of a cough and see light glaring off an iPad, giving away that someone was working nearby. The smell of freshly brewed coffee permeated the office. Voices were muffled by the door before it was opened slowly. Alan Tolsky stepped out and held the door open, motioning for Banner to enter his office.

Banner took his seat in front of Tolsky's desk and got right down to business.

"Look, Mr. Tolsky, we need a couple million bucks quick. I mean like yesterday."

"OK, that's no problem. I have a few special-interest groups in my Rolodex we can rely on. Trust me," Tolsky assured him.

"Alan, this has to be discrete. Hy-Yung doesn't want anything unethical or illegal to happen, so make sure you go through the guidelines with a fine-tooth comb," stressed Banner.

"I can assure you that the confidentiality of all my clients is my primary concern. I've been consulting politicians for decades. I have been the brain trust of more presidential campaigns than you have had birthdays. So you manage the campaign and I will raise the funds. Let me fill your war chest and you will win by a landslide."

"OK, Alan, but we need heavy-duty money."

"No problem. But my fee is ten percent on every million," returned Tolsky.

"I'm better off going to the mob."

"Look, son, that's not necessary. The insulting comments are senseless. I have some powerful contacts who are dying to get involved in the making of history. Trust me, they don't want anything in return. They're so fucking rich that they don't even count what they give me. They send me blank checks and I fill them in. That's how rich they are!" exclaimed Tolsky.

"Well, don't get me wrong, Alan. I just want to protect Hy-Yung."

"Hy-Yung is completely protected. Our contract stipulates that he and all campaign members have no knowledge of what's going on. I'm the one taking all the risk. So I do deserve my fee. And now that you insulted me, it is twenty percent above the first twenty million raised."

The men shared a solemn silence. Their mutual glances hinted at the promise of Tolsky's statement.

"Make sure you don't discuss this with Hy-Yung or anyone in the campaign, or it breaches our deal. Let's keep things quiet. Our new president has more things to worry about than the affairs of the campaign fund," Banner said.

He rose from his seat and gave Tolsky a firm handshake with direct eye contact.

After shutting the door behind him, Tolsky sat back down at his desk and picked up the phone to call Nuji.

"Hello, Nuji? Alan Tolsky here . . . Yes . . . I wanted to inform you that I just met with Hy-Yung's campaign manager and they're looking for a few million."

"Give them six million, and arrange for our stations and newspapers to give them editorial support and extra coverage," replied Nuji.

"Six million is too much at one time. I will have to route it through several different accounts and meet with all the proper people to cover our asses," said Tolsky.

"Just get me results and I will see to it that you are well rewarded."

"Nonsense, Nuji. I'm just doing my job. The only reward that I expect is my fee. Just pay five percent for each million I clean and I'm happy."

"I refuse to pay less than ten percent per million. My secretary will make arrangements for the bank wire in twenty-four hours."

"Thanks, Nuji. I am most grateful. Please let me know if there is anything I can do to help you."

Tolsky hung up the phone and called Nuji a bitch under his breath. Then he got up and walked over to his window and gazed at the busy city beneath him. The people and the cars looked like clamoring specs of dust in the distance.

***

The next day, back at the campaign headquarters, Carl Banner had an announcement to make.

"Michael, we have four million dollars in from new contributions, and we just got seven unions, fifteen governors, thirty-one senators, twenty-nine congressmen, and eleven newspapers, and more key supporters are coming in every hour. I didn't realize Alan Tolsky was this, well—powerful," Banner blurted. "I mean, whoever these backers are, they sure have a lot of influence. These people own a piece of everything."

"I know who the backers are," said Michael. "This may cause a problem in the future."

"Are they your connections from Washington? Because Alan said they would call tonight."

"No. They are old friends and new enemies."

The phone abruptly rang before Michael could say another word. Banner picked it up and motioned for Michael to come closer. Michael took the phone from him and simply said, "Nuji, stay out of my business. I don't need or want anything from you. When I win, I will only have God to thank."

"Hy-Yung, listen, I understand if you don't want help from your family or friends. I just wanted you to know that all of your friends back home are behind you one hundred percent, and we know you're going to be the best president in the history of all mankind. If you need any more support, don't call Alan, just come to me directly, because there won't be a middleman. It's just you and me from now on."

Nuji hung up, leaving a bewildered Hy-Yung staring at the phone in disbelief.

***

Three weeks passed, and election night found everyone waiting for the final results of the ballots.

An out-of-breath Carl Banner said, "Michael, all the numbers are in. It's official, we've done it—you're the president of the United States!"

"Oh God, we did it! We did it! Yeah, go ahead, Carl, get up on the podium and make it official. We've done it!"

Carl left their thirty-person entourage and took the stage to make an unrehearsed but still prepared speech.

"Ladies and gentlemen, we are proud to announce the new president of the United States of America, Michael Hy-Yung! Mr. President, we have waited on this moment for way too long. Please step up here."

Hy-Yung approached the podium and cleared his throat. "I would like to thank the people of the United States of America for voting for me, and even those who didn't, because you all represent a free democracy."

***

Kimjianta was a strong, spirited, beautiful, graceful woman with a quiet demeanor. She had graduated in the top 10 percent of her class at the Massachusetts Institute of Technology. With funding from private investors, Kim had created an intricate network of laboratories that allowed her to conduct her research and do experiments that governments and publically funded research clinics and laboratories didn't have the funding, talent, or resources to conduct. She had raised hundreds of millions of dollars over the past few years, which had benefited her young career.

Despite Kimjianta's experience and confidence being assets that made it easy for Michael to trust and respect her opinions and much needed advice, he had for years denied the funding sources and consulting assistance that she had offered him. But now Kimjianta would become a critical part of his fundraising campaign and be assigned to watching über-fundraiser Carl Banner.

***

News outlets quickly reported that the inauguration had the largest turnout in American history. The audience packing the National Mall was full of excitement and cheer, creating the atmosphere of a concert and a massive family event rolled into one, not a political event wrapping up what had been one of the most talked-about elections ever.

During the inauguration, Michael walked to the podium to be sworn in, flanked by an army of security. He took the oath of office and was sworn into the presidency.

Michael looked over at his beautiful wife and struggled to contain his emotions. Kimjianta stood emotionless, the commentators on television noting that President Hy-Yung's wife was so greatly reserved during such a momentous event. Michael took strength from her resolve and managed to look cool, calm, and collected.

Following his inauguration, Michael returned to the White House, where he would engage in an orientation with White House staff, as well as weeklong strategy sessions with his administration. A reporter called out from the crowd, "How does it feel, President Hy-Yung? You won by a landslide."

"The fact that former President Trump sent me a tweet was a compliment, I think," Michael said with a laugh, referring to ex-President Donald Trump tweeting, "I think America has a chance to stay ahead of the other stupid Country's. I sent the New President an email with directions on how to run my America. He has not returned my messages yet, but he will, and I will be right here to help guide on running our Government."

President Hy-Yung continued, "It's not a true landslide until our great nation has become one that enjoys the fruits of life—liberty and prosperity—and until that victorious day I request that you all join hands with me to help change our nation. Thank you."

The crowd erupted into a frenzy, and the band commenced its ceremonious presidential victory song.

***

Six months later, on a sunny afternoon, President Hy-Yung had just returned to a serene White House. The past week had been an incredibly busy one for the administration. The president had been traveling around the world on a goodwill mission, visiting different countries to meet their heads of state.

After this long trip, Hy-Yung and a Secret Service agent were engaging in serious conversation. President Hy-Yung was known as one of the most down-to-earth politicians the United States had ever seen. It was not unusual for him to show up at local events unannounced and drive the crowd into a mad frenzy. The president's security team had recently been advised to take extra precautions due to growing concerns regarding threats and anonymous tips given to the Justice Department.

"Mr. President, we will be taking special action to protect you from here on. There have been several threats, and we are greatly concerned."

"Well, that's nothing new. All presidents get death threats," said the newly elected president.

"That's true, but you're the first Asian ever elected, and a lot of people are enraged about having you as their leader. Let's face it, this is a sick world," replied the Secret Service agent.

"No problem. I have always dreamed of this moment, and nothing will get in my way."

***

Nuji understood that, in order to remain seated at the head of the table, she would need to get Michael Hy-Yung to deliver full access to the presidency of the United States of America on a platter to the thirsty leaders of the Asian Power League. This access was her first focus; however, the strategy shifted when her colleagues explained the value of using the president's ability to sign executive orders and influence policy.

This was the greatest acquisition on earth. Over the years, several key members of the Asian Power League had attempted to infiltrate high levels of the US government, at the federal, state, and city levels, to secure contracts through rigging bids or buying influence with senators, congressmen, or lobbyists at powerful law firms in Washington, D.C. The best the APL could hope to do was to gain information or try to use espionage or bribery to build their businesses.

If properly executed, having key members inside the White House would deliver the Asian Power League with not just unlimited access but unlimited power. Nuji had been assigned the responsibility of leveraging her relationship with friends and family to compromise the system so that the APL could gain control of the powers that be.

Nuji had virtually sold her soul in exchange for her leadership role in the organization. She understood that if she did not complete this task, her death was guaranteed. This gave her no choice but to kill or be killed. Over time, the pressure and demands on Nuji had taken a toll on her mental health and ability to make rational decisions. Her desperation left death and destruction behind her each step of the way. Michael Hy-Yung had made it clear from day one that he was not going to cooperate or assist the Asian Power League at any level or in any manner.

CHAPTER FOURTEEN

A Tender Offer

THE ROOM WAS A MESS. There were food trays and empty glasses and cans all over the place. It looked more like a college freshman's dorm than the meeting place of the people running the biggest corporation on earth—the United States government.

Carl Banner was out of breath and somewhat insistent that he and Hy-Yung sit down to discuss an urgent matter.

Carl cleared his throat and sternly said, "Mr. President, Alan Tolsky slipped in the shower and died last night. I talked with his secretary, and she said all our data on the firm's cloud has been erased and the backup hard drives are missing. Three of the best firms in the world have been trying to recover our data. Now the Justice Department is going to the Senate to request a special hearing for a full inquiry and investigation to make sure that everything was on the up-and-up with Alan."

Fortunately, the data was synched to a recovery system that tracked any additions, edits, or deletions. Thanks to Michael's tech firm managing the account, this backup system had secured everything. A data breach would have brought a level of confusion and danger that would have compromised the ability of any of the groups involved to know who initiated the attack, as well as to determine who and how much each party had benefited.

The first breach had occurred when Alan Tolsky died. That this happened additional times was a great indicator that several parties may have been involved in the cyberattack. The White House administration informed the president's chief of staff that they would monitor the situation and act on a proactive basis.

Michael was able to gain access to a detailed report on each breach, since the company was one of many he controlled through a vast network of corporate entities he owned through a triple-blind trust, created to remain compliant with laws designed to prevent conflicts of interest. This leverage enabled him to speculate on each of the possible groups that may have had an agenda or were working to gain access to this top secret information.

"I am going to talk to Nuji in a few moments. She was very involved with Alan."

"Who is Nuji, and what does she have to do with this?" asked Carl.

"Nuji is a powerful leader from an Asian organization who wants to control me. They are the ones that sent all that money to Alan, and they are responsible for the selection and recruitment of our supporters. She arranged it so we would get the right people behind us with unlimited financial resources."

"I'm really worried, Mr. President. If we are investigated or any of that data is recovered, we are fucked!"

"Carl, look into this. Try to find the secretary or look up his wife. Check his house—do something."

At that moment, Hy-Yung's chief of staff's mobile phone rang. Hy-Yung looked down and saw it was Nuji calling. He grabbed the phone and answered it. Before he could say hello, Nuji was already talking.

"Hello, Hy-Yung," she said. "Everything will be taken care of. I just want to assure you that everything we discuss will always be kept in the greatest of confidence. The Asian Power League has used its influence to help you get the necessary support to win your campaign, so try not to worry so much. Alan is no longer being retained by our organization, and all his files have been destroyed. So the only ones who know of this are, you, me, and your friend Carl Banner. But don't worry"— she laughed disturbingly—"I made sure he would honor our request for silence."

Michael's mouth hung open in awe at the sheer calmness of Nuji, admitting that she had just had his business partner murdered.

"You evil bitch! That's right, Carl does know every damn detail and all the facts. He is my witness that I knew nothing about your dirty deals, and that protects me completely!"

"Take it easy, Hy-Yung. I'm on your side. You're so damned paranoid, it's a shame. I only called to tell you I have been appointed the minister of foreign affairs to the United States."

"Good for you. How much did it cost you?" Michael yelled.

"A lot less than it cost us for you to be president."

"Fuck you, Nuji."

"Mr. President, you shouldn't talk to me that way. You have to deal with me on all official matters concerning Japan," Nuji replied calmly. "That is not professional."

"Fine. But I want you to know I'm innocent," Michael replied, and hung up.

***

Several days passed before Nuji and Michael were on the phone again.

"You're right: you are protected. And I know you have proof of your innocence. You have nothing to be worried about. But you know what, Hy-Yung? That's still not good enough for you. We put you in the White House, and you don't even want to help your friends," Nuji said slyly.

"Look, I was ahead in the polls, and all of my activities have been done properly, so I have nothing to worry about. I already filed the proper documents to inform the proper people of these strange events. This is all your problem. You did this all on your own, so you deal with it."

"I will deal with it, Hy-Yung, as soon as I talk to Carl Banner. I just want to make sure he keeps his mouth shut, so read tomorrow's paper."

"I am president of the United States of America, and I have sworn to serve this country. So do what you must. The past is the past, and I have no alliances with you. As far as I'm concerned, you are part of my past and you're invisible."

"Mr. President, check the news tomorrow. It will remind you that I will always be walking in your shadow. I'm gonna get off now, but keep watching social media and check the news.

I'll show you true power—raw power—just to remind you who you're fucking dealing with!" Nuji said, before throwing her phone across the room. It skittered off the marble and smacked into the wall.

CHAPTER FIFTEEN

The Raw Deal

A TALL, SLENDER SECRET SERVICE AGENT walked briskly into the Oval Office. His freshly cropped hair was neatly slicked down, with a few strands loosely draped over his pale forehead. He placed his iPhone on President Hy-Yung's desk for him to see the trending topics on social media.

"Mr. President, Carl Banner was killed in a car accident last night. It was a freak accident. A truck slammed into him at full speed."

"How do you know it was a freak accident? Were you there?" replied Hy-Yung.

"No, sir. But the reports said that the—"

"I don't give a damn what the reports are saying. You better know what you're talking about! Don't make an official statement until you have all the facts!"

"Yes, sir. I will look into it further."

As the agent left, Michael slammed his hand on the desk and yelled, "I'll get you, you motherfucker! I'll get you!" He could feel his entire world spinning out of control beneath him. He began to realize there was a great possibility that he was going to be betrayed or become the center of controversy.

Later that evening and still at his desk, Michael was contemplating his next move. Joining him was Mitchell Casey, a childhood friend of Michael's and one of his most trusted advisors. Mr. Casey had called an emergency meeting to brief him on the state of affairs.

"There are ten countries that are about to go into default on Thursday. If we do not collect what they owe us, we, too, will have a serious financial burden," said Mr. Casey.

"Can't we extend their credit or refinance their debt?" asked Michael.

"Mr. President, if we don't collect now, our nation will come to a halt. Federal tax revenue and government revenues will not generate enough income to continue to fund government programs and policies. Our budget deficit is so big that we will not even be able to print money to cover our losses."

"What are they planning to do about this? Have any of these countries offered any concessions?"

"They have all agreed to cooperate fully on this matter. They are all claiming it is impossible for them to make any payments. They also fear their citizens may panic and cause civil unrest. We may even have to prepare for a war. They have us in a very compromising position, Mr. President."

"What is our position?"

"Several key congressional members are putting together a plan to get our loans refinanced or repaid to reposition us as the economic superpower of the world. Get some rest, Mr. President. I will have some answers in the morning."

"Very well. Have a good night."

"Good night, Mr. President."

Michael tossed and turned, thinking through his plan to reverse the economic disaster. Late in the night, he sprang into action with a plan to issue an executive order and demand the company be sold, in order to divest himself and force the company to give him access to the data that would enable him to run scenarios that could lead to a possible solution to bring them back from the brink of disaster.

***

The next day brought about prompt results. Michael and Mr. Casey reconvened in the Oval Office to map out a plan of action.

"Give me an update on our plan of action, Mitchell. We only have twenty-four hours to resolve this, and one shot to get it right."

"As you know, Mr. President, Congress has been working nonstop. We should have been better prepared for a meltdown like this. Of course, no one expects it on their clock. They have former President Obama advising them on the measures and strategies he used to resolve the financial crisis of 2008. We will have a plan to present to the American people in a matter of hours. This administration will put together something that will save our nation. I will have it on your desk before the end of the day."

Later the same day, around six p.m., Mr. Casey excitedly called President Hy-Yung to announce that the House and Senate had reached an agreement, and they were ready to present it to the president and his cabinet. "Congratulations, Mr. President! You have just become the greatest president of all time thanks to the new Global Economic Expansion Policy—I'm sorry, let me correct that—*your* Global Economic Expansion Policy."

"Brief me on this plan, Mitchell."

"Essentially, the United States will be willing to suspend interest payments and write off the loans of the ten countries that are about to go into default with us, in exchange for a share in their governments and active ownership in all of their enterprises and operations."

Hy-Yung gasped in realization, "You mean a—"

"Yes, Mr. President, it's a partnership with no money down and the potential to become the biggest fucking joint venture in the history of all mankind!"

"Listen," barked Michael, "my plan was to offer each country a grant that would allow them access to the goods, services, and resources they need and to enroll them in a program that would allow them to reduce their debt obligation to us in lieu of them using our capacity and wealth in exchange for their needs. This would be—for lack of a better term—a one-sided barter. We give, and only get a credit toward what we are owed. Mitchell, do all the research you can on this. Check the domestic and international laws. See if there are any other options. This should be our last resort."

"Very well, Mr. President."

***

A day or so had passed, and Mr. Casey returned to the White House to brief President Hy-Yung. He entered the Oval Office with his laptop in hand.

"Come in, Mitchell. I haven't slept all night, but I've carefully considered the GEEP. This is something that must be approached with sensitivity. If nothing else, it can be developed and saved for a dire emergency. I think, if there is a collapse, then we will use this plan. But let's try to work something else out."

"Mr. President, the cabinet members have reviewed the Global Economic Expansion Policy, and after careful consideration, we support Congress's recommendation that we impose this policy. There are no alternatives. If there is a collapse this time, nothing will fix it. We need to act now."

"It is true: this would solve our problems and turn our government around. My only concern is that we use a program that will help other nations as well."

"Mr. President, we have no choice but to exercise our right to enact the GEEP. If we don't, our nation will be destroyed by economic ruin."

"True. However, this is such a drastic measure that it would sink other countries. It may even cause a war."

"Mr. President, that may be a chance we have to take."

"I will make my official decision in the morning, Mitchell."

"We may not have until tomorrow morning, Mr. President. This is a landmark decision. Follow the plan and you will become the greatest president of all time, the savior of our nation, a hero. But if you don't, they will override your veto anyway. Come on, Mr. President, let's make this dream come true."

Hy-Yung took in a deep breath and smiled at the information his comrade had shared. "I know you're right," he said. "I just never imagined this could actually happen. But go full steam. I will be prepared for tomorrow's press conference."

***

The following day, Mr. Casey knocked on the door to the Oval Office. After a minute or so, he entered the office. His clothes were wrinkled and his hair was messy. His face had stress written all over it. Mr. Casey joined Hy-Yung in the far corner of the office and said, "Mr. President, your conference is scheduled for this evening at seven o'clock. We'll go over your speech an hour before press time. We made a few edits that we need to review in depth. Also, sir, there is an urgent matter I need to brief you on."

"I will be ready, Mitchell. Now give me the bad news first."

"The State Department has just informed me that Russia has offered the countries a bailout. They offered the countries asylum from the United States."

"Asylum? From what?"

"Russia has assured them that they can get them out of this dilemma if they let the Russian government be their exclusive representative in this matter."

"What gave Russia this crazy idea?"

"I don't know, but that is not all of it, Mr. President. The Justice Department has informed me that the FBI has received some sensitive information from a trusted source: a confidential informant inside the White House."

After hearing this news, Hy-Yung appeared visibly shaken and sweat began beading across his forehead. "Keep me posted on this," he said. "It could give us an advantage."

"Why, of course, Mr. President. We have made it a priority on a need-to-know basis."

"Are there any key figures or suspicious parties involved?"

"Not to my knowledge, Mr. President. I believe this person is a high-ranking government official."

"Let's make our move and beat them to the punch. Then we can do whatever we have to do to destroy our enemy."

As Mr. Casey walked out the door, the phone rang. Jenny's voice could be heard over the intercom: "Mr. President, Miss Nuji Misheato is on the phone for you, sir."

"Nuji, do not call me here, this is my place of business," Michael said sternly into the phone.

"But, Hy-Yung, this is business. In fact, very serious business."

"Look, Nuji, I can't talk here."

"Fine, Hy-Yung. But if I were you, I would play ball before the FBI puts our government in a position that would force us to answer their questions."

"Woman, do what you have to, because I haven't done anything wrong."

CHAPTER SIXTEEN

The Plot Thickens

MICHAEL AWAKENED WITH HIS BEAUTIFUL WIFE standing over him with a concerned and confused look on her face.

"You weren't sleeping well," she explained, then asked, "What's troubling you?"

He explained that he was concerned that Nuji might have information that could compromise his presidency and their marriage. He expressed that his love for her was greater than any love he had for anything else in the world. Despite that, he was convinced that Nuji was hell-bent on becoming either the most powerful person on earth or the most scorned woman the world had ever seen.

Kimjianta assured him that nothing Nuji did could sway her from being loyal to him, her husband and the leader of the free world. Michael related the details of his trip to Japan that had forever changed his life. They embraced and spoke quietly in a dialogue that was familiar to only the two of them. They shared their thoughts and discussed several strategies they could use in different scenarios in the event of crisis, betrayal, or, worse, if the seeds they had planted brought back bitter fruit.

***

A week passed, and the American citizens were demanding an expeditious and thorough investigation into the current status of the economy and the methods President Hy-Yung used to raise some of the funds for his presidential campaign. This was also creating controversy and unrest in the White House. At a mahogany conference table on a tense afternoon, the FBI director thumbed through documents and gently pulled his glasses from his eyes, placing them on the table as he looked up at Hy-Yung and began to speak.

"Mr. President, we have reviewed a report regarding allegations of you using improper and unethical methods to raise campaign funds. After careful consideration, we have found that you are innocent, and no charges will be filed. We couldn't find anything."

"Well, my personal attorney has consulted me on all the matters that were under investigation. What were the findings regarding the Asian Power League?"

"As of now, Mr. President, there are no problems at all. However, your personal file will be left open. If any laws are broken, or if any activities you are involved in lead to any problems, we will have to deal with them accordingly," said the director, who began neatly stacking his documents.

"Well, I'm most pleased that everything is out in the open now," said Hy-Yung confidently. "But I want you to keep a close eye on Nuji."

"Mr. President, as long as there are no further problems, we can treat this as though it never happened. To be honest, someone really likes you, because you were really close to being subjected to a formal congressional inquiry."

"I must admit, I have been most fortunate," said President Hy-Yung, "but deservingly so, due to my remaining honest and transparent."

***

Eight days had passed since the FBI director's meeting with President Hy-Yung. Seated at a conference table in the J. Edgar Hoover Building, the FBI director was stacking documents into a neat pile on the oak table. The intense mood clearly signaled that the government was creating an environment that gave the ambiance of power and intimidation. It felt like independence without compromise.

Across from the FBI director sat Nuji. In an even tone, the director presented her with an ultimatum.

"If you can create a more rewarding and valuable arrangement for me, we can continue to keep our commitments to you," said the director, calmly. "However, if you can't, our business is done. Remember, this is still the most powerful nation on earth, and no one is untouchable!"

"What do you mean? I have immunity from prosecution. I hope you're not trying to frame me," Nuji replied. She had secretly cooperated with various world leaders and heads of state for years, so she knew she could always find an exit strategy in the event she broke a national or an international law.

"No, of course not. I just want to negotiate a better offer that will make everyone billions of dollars and allow us all to end up being written into history as heroes."

"OK, let's talk. I'm interested."

"Not here. Meet me at the Oak Bridge Country Club tomorrow."

"What are you talking about?" asked Nuji. "I've given you photos, tape recordings, and key witnesses on Hy-Yung's past and present. I have told you everything I know."

After a brief silence, the FBI director, avoiding eye contact, broke the silence with a few decided words: "Nuji, trust me, I am very interested and I see you have kept your word, and as long as you don't disclose any information on my past or tell the government that I am giving you sensitive information, I will be fine."

"We just want to reward you for all your hard work and being a man of your word," Nuji replied.

"Leave now and I'll contact you later."

"OK. I'll meet you tomorrow, Director."

"I have given you everything that I promised, and as long as you're loyal we will remain friends, Nuji."

"I look forward to talking to you at greater length," Nuji added. "Oh, and, Director, if you are willing to join our team, we will make you very wealthy and make sure the new leader will excuse all of your past crimes and mistakes. You just keep everything between the two of us."

"Look, I have been very good to you, Nuji. I expect you to return my kindness. As soon as I meet with my team, I will fill you in on the details. Until then, have a good day." The

FBI director rose from his seat and walked the length of the conference table, to the office door, where he exchanged a firm handshake with Nuji.

***

The next day, Nuji was brought over to the FBI director on the golf course of the country club by a caddy. Nuji sat in the golf cart, and they commenced their discussion.

The beautiful scenery of the perfectly manicured course against the picturesque, verdant forest was spoiled by the magnitude of their meeting. Who would expect them to speak of the fate of the free world in public, at one of the most elite golf resorts in the world?

"Look, Nuji," the director started, "you can put a new member of your team into the White House. With all the information you gave us on Hy-Yung, you have a perfect pathway to put someone else in the same position you put Hy-Yung in."

"I have even more unions, newspapers, radio and television stations—not to mention senators, judges, and lobbyists—in my corner. Your people have more money than God, so you can easily finance the whole operation again."

"With all the information you gave us on Hy-Yung, we can easily force him to step down. He won't know what's going on, and besides, we will help him make money in the private sector."

This all came as a welcome surprise to Nuji, who replied, "Let's set up our ground rules and create a system. Look, it's simple. Maybe I can't become the president of the United States of America, but you will run everything in a new system directly with me from my headquarters in Asia. We will run America by using you as our front man. But my team will call the shots. Together, we can control America and all of Asia. We will meet on all key issues and matters concerning these nations."

"That's great!" said the FBI director. "I don't even want to meet your team. You answer to the Asian team and I'll answer to the United States team, so we won't be compromised."

"Fair enough," Nuji acquiesced.

"Nuji, the American public wants to believe in the American dream. They really believe that the president runs the country. This whole damn thing is a television show. The politicians are just paid actors reading a script written by the people who really run this country. The only difference is the TV actors get awards and the American presidents get killed."

With a shake and a smile, they were done, and Nuji let herself out of the golf cart.

***

The following week, Nuji called and was as direct as she could be, and she was quickly transferred to the director's private line.

"Well . . . has your team accepted?" she asked.

"Everyone has approved and wants to put the new president in place. Who knows, the next president of the United States may be handpicked by a beautiful and powerful woman like you."

"Done deal, Director. You can count me in."

"Yes, ma'am. I will work on setting up the meetings and putting the wheels in motion, and you focus on setting up President Hy-Yung. Oh, and, Nuji, don't say a word about this. Not even to Mr. Casey. Trust no one. I'm your only contact on the US team."

CHAPTER SEVENTEEN

Yin and Yang

STILL UNBEKNOWNST TO MR. CASEY, the previous day's meeting between the FBI director and Nuji may as well have never occurred.

"Gentlemen, we need to make some changes in terms of our direction. The Republican Party is not what it used to be, and, frankly speaking, I believe it is time for a new era." Mr. Casey spoke with conviction to the group that had convened in the White House for a special meeting called by the FBI director.

"Mr. Casey, you're right. Public opinion polls show that the country has lost its appeal for Hy-Yung," said the director.

"That may be true, but he still has a strong following, and with all of the declension and bias, everyone is still in favor of an Asian running the country," said Mr. Casey.

"Why is that? I can't figure that out for the life of me," said the director.

"Well, the leaders of Japan, China, and several other Asian countries are strong supporters of the United States government now. They feel that the presence of an Asian president reflects respect, sensitivity, and a fair opportunity for immigrants in the United States. It's been quite a few years since an American president has turned a once-perceived nation of selfish bullies into a superpower with a heart for peace and economic growth on a global scale," said Mr. Casey.

"I would think people would be afraid of all the slant-eyed devils getting together and taking over the world," said the director with a laugh.

"I'm sure there are people who feel strongly on both sides, but the facts show that the Asian community has more voting and economic power than any other group in the United States right now," replied Mr. Casey.

"Then why don't we get another Asian and put him in office? We will control him. We need more say-so on all matters in this office. The Justice Department has named Nuji Misheato as an investor and a threat to the establishment and assigned her the name 'Unknown Entity.' Nuji was referred to me by the secretary of state of the United States of America. She has tremendous contacts and is a figurehead in Japan. She knows US politics very well. Nuji has also been friends with Hy-Yung for years, so she understands the rules of the game," said Mr. Casey.

"You know, now that I think about it, I remember reading about this Nuji Misheato. She can help us find a strong candidate for president of the United States. Maybe we should make her a business offer to help us run our country. This is only if we can be assured that she won't sell us out. Because if she does, we just assassinate her and put someone else in," said the FBI director.

"Remember, we have to be very careful. Let's sit down with her first, as soon as possible," said Mr. Casey.

"I will make arrangements to meet with her as soon as possible," said the director.

"Very well. We will meet again on this in the near future," said Mr. Casey.

***

One week later, a White House aide escorted Nuji Misheato into the secret meeting.

Mr. Casey spoke directly to Nuji as she took her seat: "Miss Misheato, the Republican Party is looking for a presidential candidate for the next election, and we will strongly consider the best candidate you present. Can you tell us whom you have in mind and why we should consider him or her?"

"I was born and raised in California, and I moved back to Japan when I was sixteen, where I received my PhD in economics. At age twenty-seven, I became the chairman of Neikoa Electronics. After ten years of service, I was appointed minister of foreign affairs. That is the position I have held for a while, and I believe that living and working in the US and Asia has given me an edge on knowing whom we should select for the leader of the free world and how to shape the world for a better tomorrow," said Nuji.

Said Mr. Casey, "Now, what we need is an American-born politician with many years of experience in politics and business. Miss Misheato is solely responsible for our relations with

Asia today. Let's put her in a position to help us select the right person to run for the highest office in the world, the president of the United States."

"This is a match made in heaven, gentlemen. I am willing to make each one of the Asian nations and all of their resources open to America," said Nuji.

"Hey, let's go for it. Start the wheels turning needed to put Miss Misheato in control. Let's find the perfect candidate to be our puppet, lock him in, and then set up the campaign immediately and talk Hy-Yung into stepping down," said the FBI director.

"As long as Hy-Yung steps down gracefully, we should be able to pull this off with no problem. Besides, I will contact all my people to ensure all the necessary elements for a sure victory at the polls," said Nuji.

"We will present the idea to Hy-Yung and then make our official announcement," said Mr. Casey.

"Miss Misheato, if you fail to carry out any of the terms of our deal, we will microwave you and anyone who attempts to rise up against us. Loyalty is our main concern here," said the FBI director.

"Gentlemen, gentlemen, please. I am committed and prepared. There is going to be a struggle between Hy-Yung and myself, but I will take care of this on my own," she said.

Nuji knew Michael Hy-Yung would never surrender the throne to someone he viewed as such an evil adversary. It was a winner-take-all strategy, and she was hell-bent on moving Hy-Yung out of the White House. She assumed she had everyone's support. Unfortunately, her overconfidence had grown into a blind obsession. This made it impossible for her to properly measure the risks and unpredictable factors that were part of overthrowing a president.

Smiles swept across the faces of the attendees.

CHAPTER EIGHTEEN

The Fork in the Road

As Michael stared in the mirror, he pulled the bottom layer of fabric down through the loop of his tie to secure it in place. The face staring back at him was that of a tired, but not broken, man. He was clean shaven, awake, and ready for the day. He heard his intercom buzzer go off and left the bathroom to answer the intercom in the hallway.

Jenny reminded the president of Nuji's scheduled arrival. After a brief pause, he replied, "Send her in."

Michael took his place at his desk and folded his hands squarely in front of him. When Nuji walked in, he rose from his seat and bowed his head, not taking his eyes off her.

They took their seats, and Nuji was the first to speak.

"Hello, Hy-Yung. I never thought that I would live to see a member of the Asian Power League in the White House."

"Nor did I, but you made it here, and I must admit that I am not glad to see you. I thought I should make that clear because I'm sure you're aware that I am not a member of the Asian Power League."

"Oh, but you are a member, Hy-Yung!"

Michael reached in a drawer and pulled out the APL membership guidelines and placed the document on the desk in front of Nuji. Puzzled, Nuji picked up the document and began reading.

"Look at article fourteen," Michael said. "It says you must be reactivated on a yearly basis in order to keep your status, and attend a meeting every two years in the motherland. So I haven't been a member for ten years."

"Well, well, you're right, Hy-Yung. But does the government know of your past involvement with us? And how would your country view that?"

"Nuji, all my activities have been documented, going back long before I took office. And, after all, the Asian Power League was once a great organization that stood for good, not evil. I never participated in any illegal activities or wrongdoing."

"What you're saying is the truth, but I don't think you want to create a situation that will bring you drama, confusion, or embarrassment."

"Nuji, I strongly suggest that you leave here and never return or contact me again. I will have no part of your schemes. You're a deranged and demented woman, in fact. It disturbs me!"

"Very well. I just came by to say hello."

"Do me a favor: just send me a postcard next time."

Michael rose and walked Nuji to the door. But before leaving Nuji had some choice words for him.

"I just came to inform you that I have informed the FBI of your past activities with us."

"That would be stupid. Your acts were criminal, not mine."

"True, but I have been granted immunity from prosecution."

"That's great, I'm really happy for you. Do you realize that I've never done anything wrong, or illegal, for that matter?"

"What you fail to realize is that the information I gave them is all documented and can be proven."

"Look, lady, I haven't done anything wrong!" exclaimed Michael.

"That's not the point, Hy-Yung. Your affiliation with us and your past activities make you look bad. Bad enough that you would have been better off doing the crime. Also, I made a deal that says my testimony will never be used against me. The highest court in this country can't touch me."

"Do what you want because I haven't broken any US law."

"Whose laws? The laws of the people who control you—the people who can and will cut your strings? Come on, man, face it! You're a puppet!"

"I have a great relationship with everyone I'm involved with," said Michael.

"Well, if anyone turns on you or wants you removed, we're the only ones that can save you." With that, Nuji turned and walked out the door. Michael watched her closely as she closed the door behind her.

***

Hy-Yung was busy at his desk in the Oval Office, thumbing through the documents he was reviewing. The rain outside could be heard lightly tapping at the windowpane. Then the phone rang.

"Mr. President, I have very bad news for you." It was Mr. Casey.

"What is it now?"

"Mr. President, I think you had better sit down, sir. You're gonna take this pretty hard."

"OK, Mitchell . . . What is it?" Michael removed his specs and placed them on top of the papers on the desk.

"Mr. President, Kimjianta was found dead at your vacation home in the Hamptons at four o'clock this morning. If the public hears about this, we're finished."

"I haven't been there in months! What the hell was she doing there? I wasn't going to meet her for another two weeks. How the hell did she get in there, anyway? Our security is tighter than Fort Knox!" Michael was angry and dumbfounded all at once.

"It looks like a setup, sir. The Secret Service found security clearance papers and a letter inviting her to meet you there last night. And there is one more problem, sir: someone forged your signature and gave false security credentials. Everything was fake."

"Mitchell, I want an all-out search! I want to know who is behind this. I want to know who killed Kimjianta and who is trying to set me up! I never wrote her any letters or gave her security clearance. She used to always go there with me!"

"Well, who knew you and Kimjianta were meeting at the vacation residence?"

"The whole fucking staff knew!"

"Then it could be anyone, sir," said Mr. Casey.

"You're a real Sherlock Holmes, Mitchell," said Michael, tearing up.

"Mr. President, we'll get to the bottom of this. I swear to you. I'll find the killer and the person behind this whole thing."

"Mitchell, spare nothing. Do whatever it takes."

"I assure you, sir, I won't let you down. I'm gonna get my best men on it. We'll turn this place upside down."

Little did President Hy-Yung know, Mr. Casey was the Judas in his administration. He had been contacted by members of the Asian Power League many times over the years but had refused to meet with them until he overheard conversations between Hy-Yung and his cousin. Using that knowledge, the APL was able to create enough doubt and fear in his mind that Michael Hy-Yung was a traitor who had gone rogue.

As time passed, Mr. Casey's envy of Michael and desire to be powerful rose to a boil and led to a hatred that had grown into betrayal.

CHAPTER NINETEEN

Checkmate

Mr. Casey walked briskly to the Oval Office. He was proud of his Secret Service men and private security team. As he reflected on the selection of his team, he walked into Hy-Yung's office to find him at his desk engrossed, as usual, in paperwork.

"Mr. President, I have your killer. We did it. We tracked down Kimjianta's murderer," said Mr. Casey, clapping his hands and sitting down in the chair next to the president's desk.

"Slow down. What findings? What the hell are you talking about?"

"We have intel that there is an ongoing plot and what we now believe to be several radical groups that may be planning your assassination. Mr. President, she was living a double life."

"Don't we all, Mitchell?"

"Well, I guess so, but if you let me explain what she was involved in and who she was dealing with, you will understand my point, sir. Let me explain."

"OK, explain."

"Mr. President, when Kimjianta was working as Mr. Yodhkhan's personal assistant at the university, she listened in on a phone conversation between Mr. Yodhkhan and other high-ranking Asian Power League officials about a power struggle with some politicians in the Japanese government. At that time, she was instructed to deliver some paperwork to Nuji Misheato after work. Little did she know that she was handing Nuji the orders for a contract killing. She must have suspected something, though, because she followed Nuji to a restaurant and saw her and a team of assassins execute three of the highest-ranking officials in the government. As Nuji made her escape, she saw Kimjianta's face and confronted her at the office in private the next day."

Mr. Casey had once again used intelligence from various CEOs who had been using two leaders of these countries to provide President Hy-Yung with critical, sensitive information, which was usually gathered by monitoring individuals and organizations that were operating in violation of US laws. Mr. Casey knew the level of potential damage that could be done to the administration.

"Go on. Then what happened?"

"Nuji pleaded with Kimjianta not to tell what she'd seen, or Yodhkhan would kill her for doing a sloppy job and eliminate Kimjianta, too, because she was a witness. Well, anyway, Nuji told her all about the Asian Power League and explained that she had to make the hit to become a *kensito*, which is the highest level of membership in the APL. Nuji would become the first woman in history to earn this position. Some members do not reach that level for more than thirty years. So this was her chance to be at the top, and she made it clear that anyone or anything that got in her way would be destroyed. She explained to Kimjianta that they could share the success if she kept this a secret," explained Mr. Casey.

"But why did she trust her? Or, for that matter, why did she make a deal with Nuji? That would make her indebted for life."

"Part of Nuji's initiation to become a kensito required her to have a human sacrifice that served her blindly, only to be killed at a later date by a high-ranking member. She was recruiting her for what she called her 'rise to power.' She would eventually become Nuji's soul offering."

"But couldn't Nuji have just killed her? What was she getting out of the deal? She could have sold her out once she got what she wanted."

"Don't you see? With Kimjianta on her team, Nuji would have the most loyal and beautiful woman in the order on her side. After all, she put her there and she was at her disposal. Nuji gave her the world in less than a day. She had money, power, political influence, and access to the most powerful people in the world. She knew she was loyal because she had nothing to lose. And besides, it was their secret. They were the only ones who could betray one another."

"Oh, I see. She figured she was as good as dead anyway after she witnessed the murders, so she agreed to the deal," Hy-Yung realized aloud.

"Exactly. You see, Mr. President, Nuji had put the world in both of their hands in a matter of hours. She had tasted the power and loved it, but there was no way out anyway. Even if she resisted the offer, she would have been dead. So she figured she would gamble for everything, and, to tell you the truth, I don't think she expected Nuji to keep her word."

"But she did, and at least long enough to collect. That explains Nuji, but how do you explain Yodhkhan? Why was Kimjianta so dedicated and loyal to him?"

"Yodhkhan's wife was a very strong woman. She knew of Yodhkhan's extramarital affairs and only put up with this because she worshipped her husband. Yodhkhan had a mistress whom he had fallen in love with, and he would meet her in secret locations. One night, Yodhkhan was driving with his mistress and they had a fatal car accident. She was seven months pregnant. However, before the mistress died, she begged him to take care of the baby if it survived. Yodhkhan hired a couple to adopt the child and raise her to his personal specifications. She had the very best that life had to offer, and Yodhkhan arranged it so the legal and medical records would make the couple look like her own parents. All records of her true identity were destroyed."

"Was the girl's name Kimjianta?"

"Yes. The baby's name was Kimjianta, and, Mr. President, she never knew that Yodhkhan was her true father."

"I thought she was, you know, trying to advance her career, or that she was, you know—in love with him."

"Oh God no. He loved his daughter, Mr. President. He would never have harmed her. She was more important to him than anything, and she loved him like a father, but never realized he was. When Nuji killed Yodhkhan's daughter, or should I say Kimjianta, there was no longer an heir to the throne. Now she had the option of either waiting for Yodhkhan's death by natural causes or killing him, too, to gain access to the throne, assuming the leadership of the entire organization. Her strategy was amazing."

"Genius," said Hy-Yung.

"By the way, Mr. President, we have all the key suspects and the main people involved. The FBI is rounding up the last of our suspects. Believe me, we have full knowledge of what's going on here. You'll be surprised at who's behind all of this mess, Mr. President."

"We have to resolve this as soon as possible. I want to know every detail and every name. Let's put a stop to this right now," said Hy-Yung.

"Mr. President, the cabinet members have decided to keep all this confidential. We've gotten approval from the Justice Department to keep this off the record."

"The public has a right to know what's going on, and they should," said President Hy-Yung.

"I'm sorry, but we have all agreed to secrecy on this matter. We agreed not to discuss this with anyone who might be a threat to the safety and the security of the United States," said Mr. Casey.

It had become easy for Mr. Casey to work against Michael Hy-Yung at this point. It had become commonplace for him to issue the now president Hy-Yung unfortunate news and one-sided opinions without it affecting his conscience.

"This country is too damn soft. We should shoot the son of a bitch. If it weren't for the well-being of the citizens of this country and this administration, I would demand the world be told about this."

"OK, you're right, Mr. President. But this one has to be our little secret. Everything is under control. We have a solution. We just need your approval."

"I will cooperate fully. I assure you, Mitchell."

"Very well. You will be briefed at tomorrow's breakfast meeting."

CHAPTER TWENTY

The Start of the Finish

IT WAS A GREAT UNDERTAKING FOR ANY ORGANIZATION, let alone a relatively small group trying to organize a full-blown sting operation focused on the president of the United States and the White House. The fact that it was a clandestine mission involving several different parties made it even more challenging.

President Hy-Yung walked into the Oval Office, where Mr. Casey was seated at the conference table with a list of his choices of potential candidates to become new members of the cabinet and the State Department. An air of tension filled the room as Hy-Yung took his seat.

"Good morning, Mr. President. We would like to give you an update on the state of affairs," said Mr. Casey.

"Very well, Mitchell. Let's just get to the bottom of this. Where is Nuji? I want to see her face-to-face. I want to see that murderer right now!" roared Hy-Yung.

"We have the killer, but I think you should try to relax. This is going to be difficult for you," said Mr. Casey.

"Mitchell, I can handle this. I won't rest until I see Nuji behind bars."

"Mr. President, Nuji did not kill Kimjianta."

"Then who did?"

"Your cousin Misu killed her, Mr. President."

"What do you mean, Mitchell? Are you crazy?"

"Misu killed her. He was madly in love with her. Misu had been jilted by Kimjianta. She refused his advances time and time again. Kimjianta was deeply in love with you. But when Misu read her diary, it told all about your secret affairs and it drove him mad."

"Dear God, how could he?"

"He told her that if he couldn't have her, no one would. He was tired of watching her give herself away. I will let you see for yourself. He's in the back room."

"Then bring him out. I want to see this for myself."

A Secret Service agent was appointed by Mr. Casey to bring Misu from the adjoining room. The agent obliged and disappeared into the room for a minute or so before returning with the unkempt and unshaven Misu. Misu avoided eye contact with everyone by keeping his head down.

"Misu, is this true? Answer me! Tell me it's a lie, dammit! Tell me!" exclaimed an enraged Hy-Yung.

"Hy-Yung, I'm sorry. I wish I were dead instead of her. I didn't mean to do it. I just couldn't take it anymore. I have watched her for years. I always loved her. She chose you over me. How could she do this to me?" returned Misu.

"Why didn't you tell me, Misu?"

"I wanted to, but you loved her so much. You were so perfect for each other, but I knew she was right for me. I just couldn't take it, cousin. I was so angry. I never meant to hurt anyone. Never. I'm just glad I didn't kill you too."

"Me?" shouted Hy-Yung. "You did, Misu. You did kill me. I'll pray for you, but you must pay for your crime."

The guards took Misu away, and a perplexed Hy-Yung gazed out the window, trying to process what he had heard.

***

The following day, a meeting that Hy-Yung had called with several key party and cabinet members, along with FBI representatives, was coming to a close. Hy-Yung asked Mr. Casey to leave him so that he could think.

"I'm sorry, Mr. President. I'm afraid that time has run out."

"What do you mean?" snapped Hy-Yung.

"Well, the Justice Department has gathered information from several witnesses. We have photos, wiretaps, and written testimony about several events that you have been involved in."

"What the hell are you talking about? Out with it, now!" exclaimed Hy-Yung.

"We are all aware of your affiliation with the Asian Power League, your affairs with Kimjianta, and your business deals with Nuji."

"Yes, OK . . . What's the point?"

"You are in violation of several laws and could be brought up on charges. We recommend that you resign from the presidency with grace and dignity. Mr. President, we will make things look very nice for you if you can just agree to our terms."

"This is an outrage! If I go down, we all go down! It's not gonna be that easy!"

"Come on, don't take it that way. We only want you to share with us."

"This is blackmail! You're better off with an assassination, Mitchell, so make your move now. Everything has been recorded. I'm wired. My people are listening to this!"

No one thought these secrets would come out, due to the timeline, global distance, and the number of people involved. Coincidentally, the sting operation was the result of the Justice Department's internal security protocol. An inquiry was made due to calculations from a quantum-based computer algorithm. The program was developed to be a tool to assist in the internal affairs division monitoring high-level White House personnel. The system had run a calculation that searched so deeply that it had profiled the president of the United States of America and the First Lady. The team that reviewed it had assumed this data was incorrect, and put the system into default mode, thus preventing any greater level of investigation of the president or any members of his inner circle. As a result, the computer performed a minor review of other possible breach-of-trust scenarios.

"Who are your people?"

"You won't know until the showdown. This is war!"

Hy-Yung stormed out of the Oval Office, and Mr. Casey ran after him. They reached the elevator that led to the president's private quarters.

"Look, there is no need to use your tapes or start a war. Our group has several candidates in mind. If you don't run for re-election, we can all shake hands and forget about this mess. Don't take this as a threat. I'm just being straight with you," Mr. Casey said.

"I will not buckle to your agenda or take part in any side-deal scandal. But if you guys no longer support me, then I will return to the private sector and to my business." Michael felt that he had only one life to live, and he believed it was best to use that life to come clean or to concede to the transfer of power.

"Thank you, Mr. President. We will do whatever is necessary to glorify your last term as president. You will forever remain a hero in the eyes of the American people. The transition will be very smooth, I assure you. I am going back to the group and informing them of our agreement."

"Do whatever you want, Mitchell. I have completed my mission."

"Mr. President, it is nothing personal. We just want to change our position. It is truly time for a new day."

"I am deeply hurt that you have betrayed me, Mitchell. But I am most grateful for all your years of service," said Hy-Yung, extending his hand for a handshake.

"I have not betrayed you, sir. I have only been honest with you. My job is to serve the office, not the president. However, I have in fact taken great care of you during your term in office. This is for the greater good."

***

Mr. Casey walked back to the Oval Office to talk to the cabinet members and the Justice Department officials.

"Gentlemen, I have talked to the president and he has agreed not to run for office again."

"Hell, I'm glad for his sake, after all. This makes it easy for everyone. The only thing we need now is a new candidate," said the FBI director.

"Gentlemen, I would like to announce our new policy advisor. She will assist us in the official selection of our new presidential candidate. We welcome Nuji Misheato, the woman who will have a major role in deciding who our next president of the United States of America will be!"

Everyone rose from their seats to applaud Nuji as she walked into the room, all smiles, and took her seat next to President Hy-Yung's desk.

Mr. Casey motioned for everyone to join her at the desk, where he called Hy-Yung on speaker phone. They were in for a surprise, as Hy-Yung had some vital information on the state of affairs.

"Gentlemen, you don't know this, so, as your fearless leader, I will inform you."

"Why, thank you, Mr. President," replied Mr. Casey.

"Nuji is not qualified to be president of this country. She is a citizen, but she has committed so many crimes and is about to be arrested for and convicted of murder. Her rap sheet is so long that it's on microfilm. Personally, I don't think she is a good candidate because of her involvement in several crime organizations."

"Nuji, is this true?" asked Mr. Casey.

"Well—I—we can—"

"Gentlemen, I'm calling you from Air Force One, so I'll be brief. Because of the change in your hearts, I'll be a lame duck. But if Nuji becomes president, we will all be dead ducks."

"Mr. President, what do you think we should do about this?" asked Mr. Casey.

"It's in your hands now. I am in the process of rebuilding my private organization and personal life. By the way, there is a one-hundred-million-dollar reward being offered by a few countries for the capture and arrest of Nuji Misheato. That reward would sure help the fiscal budget."

At that moment, Nuji tried to get up and walk away casually, but three Secret Service agents restrained her.

"Listen, all these matters have been resolved. They don't want me anymore. Trust me, it's all been cleared up."

"Check her fingerprints and run a code-fifteen clearance check," said Hy-Yung.

"Very well, Mr. President. Mr. Greenwall, please take Nuji for a quick verification of these allegations," said Mr. Casey.

"Just make Nuji an offer before you extradite her and she'll turn in every criminal in her network," said Hy-Yung.

The FBI director and a group of Secret Service agents took Nuji away.

"Well, Mr. President, I'm glad we have all come to terms. If this information is true, we will select a candidate among us, and of course we will keep you informed every step of the way. Our door will always be open to you," said Mr. Casey.

"Thank you, gentlemen. I'm headed back to D.C. now for a debriefing so that I'm prepared to exit after my term is completed. I'll be in the private sector. Who knows, maybe we can make money together one day," said Hy-Yung.

Everyone in the office laughed.

At that moment, the FBI director returned to the office and handed Mr. Casey a printed report, which he took a few moments to read.

"Mr. President, you were right. Nuji is wanted in eleven countries under different names. The reward is much higher than a hundred million dollars. I hope you understand that when we wanted her to assist us in finding a replacement for you, it was only because we believed she was a good candidate. I hope you don't feel betrayed. It was just a mistake, but no love lost, right?"

"Please, you're welcome to call me anytime, Mitchell," said Hy-Yung. He paused and took a deep breath.

"Mr. President, are you all right?"

"Yes, I'm just looking at the view of the Pentagon from the air," Hy-Yung said. He hung up as Air Force One prepared for landing.

***

The presidential limo pulled up in front of the Pentagon. As Hy-Yung climbed out of the limo and headed to the entrance, he was flocked by the press, who were all clamoring to get to him.

A reporter called out, "Mr. President, can you give us a statement on the reason for this meeting at the Pentagon?"

"I will not be running for another term as president of the United States. We are setting things up for the new administration, for a new transition."

Another reporter called out, "Mr. President, you have had a profound effect on politics and life here in the US as well as the world. What is your role in world politics now?"

"I will always be open for any forum or questions that will shape and guide our great nation and the world."

"Mr. President, do you have anyone in mind to replace you? Who will you endorse?" called out another reporter.

"Not at this time, no."

As Hy-Yung reached the top of the Pentagon steps, he turned to answer one more question before going inside.

"Mr. President, all our great presidents have made a statement at the end of their terms. What statement can you make that reflects your experience as president?"

Michael Hy-Yung focused on something in the distance. Slowly raising his hand, he pointed to the eastern sky. "Ladies and gentlemen, the sun has risen. It's a new day now."

CPSIA information can be obtained
at www.ICGtesting.com
Printed in the USA
JSHW012200140920
7907JS00002B/87